OBSCURITY

PROS AND CONS

BOOK 5

CHRISTY BARRITT

River Heights

CHAPTER 1

ELEVEN YEARS AGO, BLUE RIDGE MOUNTAINS, GEORGIA

Fourteen-year-old Olive Sterling adjusted her backpack straps as her father gathered the family at their campsite. As the early morning sun shone down on them, Dad's eyes were bright with the kind of excitement that usually meant trouble.

"Listen up, Sterling family adventurers." Dad used the theatrical voice he reserved for special occasions. "This isn't just any camping trip. We're going on a real treasure hunt."

The twins—Jessie and Jules, eight years old and still young enough to believe in magic—squealed with delight, bouncing on their toes like springs. Even Mom looked up from applying sunscreen, curiosity replacing her usual anxiety, which had become more pronounced over the past year.

"What kind of treasure, Daddy?" Jessie asked, her gap-toothed grin infectious as she grabbed Jules's hand in excitement.

"The best kind."

Olive waited for him to continue. He'd told the family this morning to pack up, and she'd halfway expected him to tell them they were moving again.

Instead, he'd brought them to this campground in the middle of the mountains.

The twinkle in his eyes scared her the most.

She'd seen the look before, and it never led anywhere good. It meant he had something up his sleeve.

Dad spread an official-looking topographical map across the weathered picnic table at the site. The morning sun caught the edges of the paper, making it glow with possibility.

"Back in the 1860s, a wealthy plantation owner named Cornelius Slattery fled north with his family fortune as General Sherman's army approached," Dad started. "Legend says he buried three chests of gold coins somewhere in these mountains, planning to return after the war."

Olive studied the map, noting the hand-drawn X marks and faded notations that looked authentically old but somehow too convenient. The aged paper had just the right amount of yellowing, the ink appeared properly faded, and the geographic details matched their current location with suspicious precision.

"How do you know about this treasure, Dad?" She narrowed her eyes as she studied one of the marked trails.

"Research, sweetheart. Months and months of careful research."

Dad pulled out a leather portfolio filled with what appeared to be photocopied documents—letters written in spidery handwriting, land deeds with official-looking seals, even what looked like pages from old journals.

"I've been corresponding with historians at the University of Georgia, tracking down his old family letters and mining records," he continued. "It turns out Cornelius was smarter than most. He left clues."

Mom moved closer to Dad, examining the papers. Her fingers traced the edges of one document, and Olive caught her slight frown.

"These look very . . . detailed," Mom said. "And remarkably well-preserved for documents that are supposedly over a century old."

"They are copies, of course." Dad grinned, his tone suggesting Mom's observation was perfectly natural. "The originals are in climate-controlled archives. But these reproductions capture every detail."

"Keep going," Mom gave up applying sunscreen

and crossed her arms instead as she waited for Dad to continue.

"Slattery was an educated man—studied engineering at the University of Virginia. He knew his family might not survive the war, so he created a treasure map that could be followed by anyone intelligent enough to solve his riddles."

Jules tugged on Dad's shirt sleeve. "Are we going to be rich, Daddy?"

Dad crouched down to meet her eyes. "Well, that depends on how good we are at following clues and working together as a team. Treasure hunting isn't just about luck—it's about using your brain, paying attention to details, and never giving up."

Olive felt the familiar mixture of excitement and skepticism that always accompanied her father's grand schemes. The documents looked real—aged and authentic in a way that would fool most people.

The story sounded plausible. She'd studied enough Civil War history to know that wealthy Southerners had indeed fled north with their valuables. And the twins were already chattering about what they'd do with their share of the treasure, their voices bright with the kind of hope that made Olive's chest ache.

But something in Dad's tone—too rehearsed, too perfect—made her wonder if Cornelius Slattery had ever existed at all. Olive had watched her dad practice stories before. She'd seen how he could weave together historical facts with complete fiction until even she couldn't tell where truth ended and invention began.

"What makes you think the treasure is still here?" Olive swatted away an annoying fly that had been buzzing around her since they arrived. "If this map has existed for way over a hundred years, wouldn't someone have found the treasure by now?"

Dad's smile widened, as if he'd been hoping for that question. "Excellent thinking, Ollie. You're absolutely right—if this were a widely known treasure map, it would have been found decades ago. But here's the beautiful part . . ."

She waited, hardly able to breathe.

Even though she was wise to her father's ways, part of her still wanted to believe what he told her.

That made her a fool.

He leaned forward as if sharing a secret, drawing the whole family into his circle of influence. "The clues weren't all in one place. Slattery was paranoid about his hiding spot being discovered, so he scattered pieces of the puzzle across different locations and with different families."

He pulled out another document, this one appearing to be a letter written in different handwriting.

"This piece came from the descendants of Slattery's business partner. This one"—he indicated a hand-drawn map fragment—"was found in the personal effects of a Union soldier who may have encountered Slattery during his flight north. I've spent two years tracking down all the pieces and putting them together."

"Two years?" Mom's voice lilted with surprise. "You never mentioned—"

"I didn't want to get everyone's hopes up until I was certain," Dad said. "You know how these historical mysteries can be. False leads, dead ends, documents that turn out to be forgeries. But last month, when I found the final piece of the puzzle, everything clicked into place."

He spread the documents across the table like a dealer revealing a winning hand. Maps, letters, sketches, and what appeared to be geological surveys—all pointing to the same general area where they were currently camping.

Olive watched her mother's expression soften as she examined the evidence. Mom had always been the skeptical one, the voice of reason that balanced Dad's wilder schemes. But even she seemed caught up in the careful presentation, the weight of apparent historical evidence.

"It's quite a coincidence that our family camping trip just happens to be in the exact area where this treasure is hidden." Olive decided to test the boundaries of her father's story.

Dad laughed, the sound genuine and warm.

"Coincidence? Sweetheart, this isn't a coincidence at all. I've been planning this camping trip specifically to search for Slattery's treasure. Why do you think I was so insistent we come to this particular campground, in this particular valley?" He gestured to the mountains surrounding them. "Everything has been carefully calculated."

The explanation was smooth, logical, and completely believable. Which, Olive began to realize, was exactly what made it so suspicious.

"So we're really going to dig for buried treasure?" Jessie asked, her eyes wide with wonder.

"We're going to follow the clues wherever they lead us," Dad confirmed. "It might be buried treasure, or it might be hidden in a cave, or tucked away in some old mining equipment. Slattery was clever—he would have chosen a hiding place that could survive decades of weather and wouldn't be accidentally discovered."

Jules raised her hand as if she were in school. "What if we don't find it?"

"Then we'll have learned something valuable about history, about these mountains, and about working together as a family," Dad said. "But I have a very good feeling about our chances. The clues all point to this area, and we have advantages that previous treasure hunters didn't have."

"Like what?" Olive asked.

Dad's grin turned mysterious. "Like modern technology, better maps, and most importantly—" He paused dramatically, letting the anticipation build. "Like having the smartest, most determined treasure hunting team in Georgia."

The twins giggled and high-fived each other, their excitement infectious. Even Mom was smiling now, caught up in the adventure despite her earlier skepticism.

But Olive found herself studying the documents more carefully, noting inconsistencies in the aging, similarities in handwriting that suggested a single author, and references that seemed just a little too convenient.

Her father was good—better than good—but she was learning to see through his performances.

Even if Cornelius Slattery was fictional, even if the treasure hunt was an elaborate game, the excitement on her family's faces was real. The sense of adventure, of working together toward a common goal, of believing in something magical—that had value beyond any buried gold.

Maybe that was the real treasure her father was

after. Maybe the story itself was worth more than whatever con he was actually planning.

Or maybe Olive was just getting better at recognizing when she was being manipulated, even by someone she loved.

CHAPTER 2

PRESENT DAY

Olive Sterling stared out the windshield at the winding West Virginia road, her knuckles white against the steering wheel. She watched as the mist clung to the mountains like secrets refusing to be told.

She knew all about secrets. They were what she did best.

This week, she needed to discover information these mountains already knew.

The engine of her 91 Jeep Wagoneer hummed steadily beneath her as she navigated another sharp curve. But the familiar sound did nothing to calm the nervous energy thrumming through her veins.

In just over an hour, she'd be seeing Jason Stewart for the first time since he'd joined Aegis three weeks ago.

In those weeks, she'd successfully managed to avoid him. He'd been away on assignment, and when he returned she was gone, and vice versa.

Now, they were going to have to see each other. Work with each other.

Pretend to be married.

And she wasn't sure she was ready.

But this case required both of them, and there was no avoiding him anymore. He would leave his current assignment and meet her at the lodge a little later.

She was a professional and could handle this. That was what she kept telling herself at least.

The sun was sinking behind the ridgeline, casting long shadows across the narrow ribbon of cracked asphalt that wound through the mountains like a scar. What had started as a proper two-lane highway hours ago had gradually deteriorated into something barely wide enough for two vehicles to pass.

The pavement was pitted with potholes that could swallow a tire, and in some places, chunks of roadway had crumbled away entirely, leaving jagged edges where the mountain had reclaimed its territory.

On her left, the road dropped away into a steep ravine choked with rhododendron and mountain laurel. Their dark leaves created an impenetrable wall of green that seemed to swallow sound.

On her right, weathered rock face rose at an impossible angle, streaked with rust-colored minerals and crowned with scraggly pine trees that clung to impossible handholds. Every few hundred yards, loose gravel cascaded down the slope, pinging against her windshield like warnings.

The guardrails—where they existed at all—were ancient things of rusted steel and rotting wood posts that looked like they'd collapse if a strong wind hit them. Most of the curves were blind, forcing her to creep around each bend while hoping nothing was coming from the opposite direction.

This wasn't the kind of scenic mountain drive featured in tourism brochures—this was backcountry wilderness that felt more abandoned than picturesque, the kind of place where a breakdown could leave you stranded until morning.

Her phone rang on the holder on the dash, the screen displaying "Rex Blackwood." Her boss. He was probably checking in one last time before she went dark for the weekend.

She hit the button, putting the phone on speaker.

"Sterling here." She kept her eyes on the increasingly treacherous mountain road as she answered.

"Olive, I just wanted to—" Rex's voice cut out, and harsh static filled the line.

She winced at the sound. "Rex, are you still there?"

"We're getting reports of—"

More static.

Then silence.

"Rex? Can you hear me?" She glanced at her phone's display.

She had two bars, but the call had dropped.

She tried calling back, but the phone wouldn't connect.

Spotty mountain reception most likely. What had he been trying to tell her?

Maybe he'd try again later, especially if it was important.

For now, Olive kept driving, mentally reviewing her persona for the weekend and all the details she needed to keep straight.

She hit the Play button on her phone screen, and music began drifting through her phone's speaker. The band was Obscurity, ironically a group she'd never heard of before this assignment.

They had a strong following with their country-rap infusion. Personally, their songs hurt her ears. But she would have to endure this music all week-end, and she had to act like she liked it.

She needed to be able to sing along, to act like a super fan.

It was all in the job description.

She hummed along.

Down in the holler where the shadows grow long

There's whispers in the wind of something gone wrong

They say don't go walking when the moon gets thin

'Cause some folks who wander don't come back again

These mountains got secrets buried deep and dark

They'll swallow your soul and leave barely a mark

So listen real close to what the old folks say

Some places are meant to stay hidden away

A few minutes later, her GPS announced a detour due to road construction. The new route directed her off the backroad she was on and onto an even more narrow mountain road.

Her jaw hardened as she gripped the steering wheel more tightly. A detour hadn't been on her schedule, but she was at the mercy of technology right now.

A few minutes later, the pavement gave way to gravel. Then a quarter of a mile later the road turned into something barely wider than a logging trail that wound through increasingly dense forest. Over time, heavy rainfall had left its mark, creating deep ruts in the rugged road.

This couldn't be right. She checked the GPS again.

The device still insisted she was on the correct route to Pine Ridge Lodge.

Tension stretched between her shoulder blades.

She'd go a little farther, and if this road didn't get any better, she would turn around.

After another ten minutes of progressively questionable navigation, she spotted her first sign of life.

A small, weathered gas station squatted beside the road like a forgotten monument to better times. The building itself was a study in decay—white clapboard siding that had faded to the color of old bones, with paint peeling away in long strips that curled like dead skin. The roof sagged in the middle, where decades of snow and rain had taken their toll, and several shingles had slipped loose, hanging at odd angles or missing entirely.

The concrete pad around the building was cracked and stained with motor oil, creating dark abstract patterns that looked almost deliberate. Weeds pushed up through every fissure, and an old metal sign advertising a long-defunct motor oil brand was riddled with bullet holes.

A hand-painted sign reading "Murphy's Last Stop" hung from a single chain, the faded red letters barely visible against wood that had weathered to silver-gray. Below it, a smaller placard promised "Cold Beer • Hot Coffee • Bait," though the paint was so faded it was hard to make out the words.

Two pickup trucks sat parked outside, which indicated the place was actually operational despite its decrepit appearance. One was a rusted Ford with a Confederate flag decal and the other a newer Chevy with mud-caked wheel wells.

Maybe a nice older man whose family had lived in this area for generations, who exuded Southern hospitality and warmth, was working inside and wouldn't mind answering her questions. People were more helpful out in the country, right? And since she was in West Virginia, Southern hospitality should be in full swing.

Olive pulled to a stop and parked in the gravel lot.

She'd go inside, ask for directions, and hopefully still arrive at the lodge in time to meet Jason.

Detours hadn't been on her schedule. But sometimes, they were inevitable.

The bell above the door chimed as Olive entered, and she was hit by the smell of stale cigarettes, motor oil, and something indefinably sour.

Was that alcohol of some sort?

Her instincts immediately went on alert.

She wasn't afraid of being in the backwoods. Of being an outsider.

She'd lived the life of an outsider, so she was used to it.

But something about this place felt a little too backward for her tastes.

She quickly scanned the store. A single glass-fronted refrigerator with drinks inside. Several displays of snacks. A wall of cigarettes.

The floor was stained. The ceiling tiles had water marks or were missing altogether. Everything was dirty, covered in years of dust and grime.

Two men stood near the beer cooler. Their conversation stopped when she walked in.

Both men were probably in their forties and wore work clothes that had seen better days. Baseball caps were pulled low over their faces, and the shorter one had a bushy beard. The taller one had pale eyes that tracked her movement with uncomfortable intensity.

Her instincts screamed for her to leave.

"Help you?" The clerk behind the counter was an older man with grizzled features and suspicious eyes.

He didn't exude the Southern hospitality Olive had hoped for. Instead, he gave off a hunting vibe—but not in a good way.

It was in a way that indicated she could be the prey.

"Good evening. I'm trying to get to Pine Ridge Lodge." Olive kept her voice friendly despite the prickle of unease between her shoulder blades. "My GPS took me on some kind of detour, and I think I'm lost."

"Pine Ridge, huh?" The clerk's expression didn't change, but something shifted in the atmosphere of the small store. "You here for that music thing?"

"That's right. Just a weekend getaway." She pulled out her phone, hoping to show him the route she'd been following. "My phone's acting up, though. I can't seem to get online."

"Yeah, reception ain't great around here." The clerk stared at the map on her phone. "Pine Ridge is about thirty minutes back the way you came, then left on County Road 15. Can't miss it."

"There's no road construction?"

He shrugged. "Not that I've heard about."

Thirty minutes back? This detour had put her seriously behind schedule.

She was about to ask for clarification when one of the men by the beer cooler spoke up.

"Another one heading to Grayfall." Though he was speaking to his companion, his gravelly voice carried in the small space. "They don't know what they're in for."

Olive wasn't sure if he was playing with her, trying to scare her away, or both. His tone was impossible to read.

"Too many people asking questions about that

place," the other man said. "They're about to find out what kinds of things happen there."

She glanced back. She'd felt the man's eyes on her since she stepped inside—and they weren't always on her face either.

"Some folks need to learn to stay away from places where they don't belong," Pale Eyes continued.

The words were clearly meant for her to hear. They were a warning, delivered in a way that suggested these men were used to making people uncomfortable. Maybe they even enjoyed it.

Olive maintained her friendly demeanor while keeping her eye on the exit and noting the exact positioning of everyone in the store.

Over her shoulder, she noticed that Pale Eyes had shifted toward the door.

She needed to get out of here. Now.

"Well, thanks for the directions." Her voice carried just the right note of cheerful gratitude while her fingers curled slightly at her sides, ready to react.

The smile she offered was perfectly calibrated—wide enough to seem genuine, but not so broad as to appear nervous. Her shoulders remained relaxed despite the adrenaline coursing through her system, and she kept her breathing steady and controlled even as she memorized the exact distance to each potential threat.

She headed toward the exit with measured steps that looked casual but kept her balanced and ready to react.

She was almost to the door when Pale Eyes shuffled around her and stepped directly into her path, close enough that she could smell stale beer and tobacco on his breath.

"Maybe you didn't hear us." His voice was low and threatening as he grabbed her arm. "Some places ain't meant for outsiders. But we could make an exception for you. Maybe make a deal."

Her skin crawled as he looked her up and down. "What kind of deal?"

He grinned as if victorious and stepped closer. "Why don't you let me show you a good time?"

Behind him, his friend hooted in encouragement.

Olive's stomach roiled with disgust. This place wasn't meant for out-of-towners. It was only for locals—and maybe not all locals. Some locals probably knew better than to come in here.

She'd made a serious mistake by coming inside.

She looked at the man leering at her.

Then every muscle inside her coiled like a spring ready to unleash.

CHAPTER 3

Pale Eyes reached for her.

As he did, Olive caught his wrist and twisted it sharply to the left while stepping back with her right foot.

The leverage sent him stumbling forward, off-balance and cursing.

Before he could recover, she pivoted behind him and applied pressure to the nerve cluster at the base of his neck with her thumb.

"Touch me again, and you'll be eating through a straw." Her voice carried a calm authority that came from years of professional experience. She increased the pressure just enough to make him gasp. "Are we clear?"

"What in the world, lady—"

She released him with a small shove that sent him

stumbling toward the beer cooler, his boots scraping against the linoleum as he fought to regain his balance.

The second man started forward, his face flushed with anger and embarrassment for his friend.

But he stopped dead when he noticed Olive's stare. She made sure that her eyes held a cold challenge. Made sure her stance remained perfectly balanced with hands loose at her sides but ready.

She dared him to give her a reason to demonstrate her skills again.

He took a step back instead.

Smart man.

"Gentlemen." Olive straightened her shoulders with deliberate calm, brushing an imaginary speck of dust from her sleeve as if the entire encounter had been nothing more than a minor inconvenience. "Thanks again for the directions. I'm sure we won't have any more misunderstandings."

The bell chimed as she walked out. She kept her movements unhurried despite the adrenaline coursing through her system.

Whatever she did, she couldn't show fear. If she did, these men might come back for round two.

Behind her, Pale Eyes cursed, and his friend told him to "let it go."

Wise advice.

She scanned the area for additional threats. The

gravel parking lot was empty except for the two pickup trucks she'd seen when she arrived.

There was no movement in the trees that pressed close against the back of the building. No other buildings where someone could be watching from cover.

The narrow mountain road stretched empty in both directions, disappearing around curves that could hide approaching vehicles but showed no signs of current traffic.

Only when she was back inside her Wagoneer and on the gravel road did she allow herself to relax.

That encounter had lasted less than ten minutes, but it had shaken her and had left her feeling off her game.

If she hadn't had the skills she did . . . she didn't want to think about what that man might have done.

The reality also remained that she may have blown her cover. She'd had no choice, however. Now she only prayed those men didn't have any connection to the festival.

She backtracked to County Road 15—the same direction she'd initially come from.

But as she eased onto the road, she couldn't shake the feeling she was being watched.

She knew men with egos didn't appreciate being put in their place and might want vengeance. Had one of the men from the gas station followed her?

Every time she checked her rearview mirror, an empty road stretched behind her. But the sensation of being watched persisted like an itch she couldn't scratch.

She'd need to keep her eyes wide open.

Those men and the trouble they brought with them were a distraction she couldn't afford. Because with every passing second, Chloe Kingston could be getting farther and farther away.

Olive prayed Chloe hadn't encountered any men like those at the gas station.

As Olive drove toward the lodge, Miles Kingston's voice played in her memory: "Any word? It's been a week since we heard from Chloe. Please, tell me you've found something."

The man had been calling her every day, ever since he'd hired Aegis four days ago.

The tech billionaire's twenty-four-year-old daughter had vanished while helping to plan and set up the inaugural Grayfall Music Festival in the abandoned mining settlement of Grayfall.

Chloe had been one of the lead organizers, hired to handle logistics and artist relations for what was supposed to be an intimate weekend of underground music.

The last communication anyone had received from her was a text that made Olive's skin crawl every time she read it.

There's more to Grayfall than you think. The trees are watching.

The trees are watching? What did that mean?

Olive couldn't stop asking herself that question ever since she'd seen the text.

Local authorities had insisted Chloe was an adult who'd simply decided to skip town after the stress of organizing such an ambitious event.

But Chloe's family knew better.

Chloe wouldn't just vanish into thin air, leaving behind her responsibilities and her entire life.

For the past three days, Olive had immersed herself in research about the Grayfall festival and everyone connected to it. What she'd discovered had only deepened her concerns about what Chloe might have stumbled into.

Grayfall was the brainchild of Brad Kellerman, a man whose entrepreneurial history read like a cautionary tale of failed ventures and questionable business practices.

His previous attempts at event management had left a trail of unpaid vendors, disappointed investors, and mysteriously canceled performances. Yet somehow, he'd managed to secure funding for an ambitious three-day festival featuring twenty fringe bands in one of the most remote locations in West Virginia.

The festival promised an authentic experience for a cozy group of five hundred music enthusiasts willing to pay premium prices—nearly five thousand dollars per ticket—for the privilege of camping in an abandoned mining town and listening to live music.

Food vendors, craft booths, and "immersive historical experiences" were all part of the package, along with performances by bands Olive had vaguely heard of in underground music circles. The event was adult-only and promised to be unforgettable.

What made her most suspicious was the logistics.

The old town of Grayfall had been cut off from vehicular access several years ago when flooding washed out the main road leading into town. Since the settlement had been abandoned for decades, no one had bothered to repair the infrastructure.

The only way to reach the festival grounds was on foot—a grueling hike that would challenge even experienced outdoor enthusiasts.

Kellerman had arranged parking near the lodge. A shuttle would take them as far down the trail as possible, but attendees would still have to hike five miles to Grayfall. Most festivalgoers would only need to bring a backpack with toiletries and clothes. Everything else would be provided.

Who chooses to hold a festival somewhere people can barely reach? Olive wondered, her unease from the gas station encounter adding new weight to the question. *And why are people willing to pay so much for such an inconvenient experience?*

Things didn't add up in her mind.

She needed to find answers.

But being in such an isolated place would make all of this complicated . . . and entirely more dangerous.

CHAPTER 4

In the process of researching the festival, Olive had discovered that two other people had gone missing in this area within the past month—people not necessarily associated with Grayfall, but who'd been in the vicinity.

The first was David Brooks, a thirty-four-year-old software engineer from Richmond, Virginia, who loved hiking. His car had been found at a trailhead parking area twelve miles from Grayfall. David was an experienced hiker who always filed detailed trail plans with park rangers. But he'd never checked in from his planned overnight campsite.

The second disappearance was even more unsettling. Clara Holloway, a sixty-seven-year-old retired botanist from Virginia Tech, had been conducting research on rare mountain plants for the state environmental agency. Her colleagues described her as methodical and safety-conscious, someone who'd spent forty years hiking these mountains without incident. Her field notebook, found beside a creek bed three days after she was reported missing, contained her usual meticulous observations right up until the final entry. *Something wrong here. Animals too quiet. Going back to truck.*

Both had vanished without a trace.

The pattern was troubling, and it suggested that whatever had happened to Chloe might be part of something larger and more dangerous than a random missing person case.

A flash of something in Olive's rearview mirror made her pulse quicken.

When she looked more carefully, the road behind her was empty.

It was probably just shadows and paranoia.

But the men at Murphy's Last Stop had made it clear that too many people were asking questions about Grayfall. Some people around here had to know what was going on.

Olive needed to find those people.

She and Jason were going undercover as music enthusiasts attending the festival. They'd pose as a married couple from Ohio who were interested in the underground music scene. For this weekend, they would be Jase and Olivia Jones—sticking close to their real first names was always helpful. Jase was a contractor, and Olivia had developed her own line of all-natural soaps and lotions.

She'd already transformed her appearance into that of someone who fit the festival demographic: non-synthetic fabrics, braided hair, minimal makeup, and the lingering scent of patchouli oil.

The persona felt comfortable, reminiscent of the many identities she'd worn growing up when her family was constantly moving, constantly reinventing themselves for her father's various schemes.

Olive checked behind her again, watching for anyone following.

There was still no one.

That should make her feel better. So why didn't it? Maybe it was because this whole case was filled with mountain lore, ghost stories, and imminent danger.

Finally, a sign appeared in front of her. "Pine Ridge Lodge—2 Miles."

Pine Ridge was a huge lodge located in the middle of the West Virginia wilderness. Years ago, it had been a hunting lodge. Today, it was mostly used for corporate retreats where people wanted to go off-grid.

The lodge was the base of operations for the weekend, the staging area where festivalgoers would gather before making the trek to Grayfall. Jason was supposed to meet her here. Tevin McIntyre, another colleague, was also coming along.

As she crested the hill, the building came into view—a massive log structure that looked like it belonged in a tourism brochure. A hand-carved sign reading "Pine Ridge Lodge" hung above the entrance, flanked by carved bears that seemed to watch approaching visitors with wooden eyes.

Olive pulled into the parking area, already noting the mix of vehicles—expensive SUVs with roof racks alongside beat-up Subarus covered in bumper stickers proclaiming various environmental causes and other music festivals.

It was exactly the kind of eclectic combination she expected at an underground music event that attracted both trust-fund hippies and genuine counterculture enthusiasts.

As soon as she climbed from the Wagoneer, she shouldered her backpack.

Her heart hammered against her ribs as she thought about seeing Jason.

Keep it professional, she reminded herself. *You're here to find a missing girl, not to rehash ancient history or let some local thugs intimidate you.*

But as she walked toward the lodge's entrance, Olive knew that some conversations could only be avoided for so long.

In her experience, the most dangerous secrets

were often hidden behind the most welcoming smiles. And in a place laden with mystery, everyone was a suspect until proven otherwise.

Including the man she'd once loved, who was about to walk back into her life whether Olive was ready or not.

Pine Ridge Lodge's interior felt almost too perfect—as if someone had consulted a handbook on "How to Create the Ideal Mountain Retreat" and followed it to the letter.

Exposed timber beams stretched across vaulted ceilings, while a massive stone fireplace dominated the far wall, its hearth crackling with a fire that seemed unnecessary given the warm June weather.

Leather furniture arranged in conversational clusters invited guests to linger, and the air carried the scent of evergreen and something else—something that reminded Olive of the sanitized smell of a doctor's office.

"Welcome to Pine Ridge Lodge!" A man emerged from behind the reception desk with the kind of smile that belonged in a toothpaste commercial. "You must be Mrs. Jones. I'm Elias Mercer, the owner."

Olive paused and adjusted the strap of her backpack. She hadn't given her name yet, and while it was possible Elias had seen her reservation—and her photo—something in his tone suggested he'd been expecting her specifically—that she wasn't merely a guest checking in.

Maybe it was paranoia after the gas station incident.

But maybe it wasn't.

She quickly observed the man.

Elias Mercer was probably in his mid-forties, and he had the kind of outdoorsy good looks that belonged on a tourism brochure. His thick, dark hair had already grayed at the temples. His tan suggested he'd spent just enough time in the sun without looking weathered. His flannel shirt was pressed, and his hiking boots appeared expensive but pristine.

Everything about his appearance felt curated rather than authentic.

Olive offered a professional smile as she looked at him. "My GPS took me on a little detour on the way here."

"Sometimes those things go a little wonky in this area," Elias said. "You're not the first person who's said that." He glanced beyond her. "Is your husband with you?"

"He's arriving a little later. We're looking forward to Grayfall this weekend. We understand you also have some excellent hiking trails nearby. If we have any free time, we definitely want to explore them."

"The best in West Virginia, if I do say so myself. Though I trust you'll stick to the marked trails. There have been some . . . unfortunate incidents with folks who venture too far off the beaten path."

The way he said "unfortunate incidents" made it sound like he was discussing minor inconveniences rather than missing persons.

"Of course."

"And there are bears as well as the occasional mountain lion."

"Sounds . . . dangerous."

"Not if people follow directions." The threatening words sounded less dangerous with his pleasant tone and smile.

But Olive stored the warning away in the back of her mind. Until she knew what kind of people she was dealing with, she needed to tread carefully.

She glanced around the main room. "It looks like you have quite a few guests going to the music festival."

Elias followed her gaze. "I've been amazed by the turnout. We're fortunate to have such dedicated music enthusiasts who are willing to travel to this area for the festival."

"Speaking of this area . . . I'd love to hear more about its history," she said. "I understand the music festival is being held in an old mining town. Is that correct?"

Elias's smile faltered for a fraction of a second. "Grayfall. Yes, it's . . . historically significant. You'll get to see the place firsthand for yourself tomorrow. I don't want to spoil any of the surprises."

She wasn't so sure she wanted to be surprised.

"Now, let me show you to your room," Elias continued. "I'm sure you want to get settled so you can get some rest before the music festival."

Yes, she did need to get some rest.

Olive needed to be sharp if she didn't want to end up as another unexplained disappearance that would haunt these mountains forever.

CHAPTER 5

Olive's room was located on the second floor overlooking the back of the property, where the manicured grounds gave way to dense forest. Through the window, she spotted a maintenance shed partially hidden among the trees, and beyond that, a trail that disappeared into the woodland shadows.

The accommodations themselves were comfortable—a king bed with a handmade quilt, a writing desk positioned near the window, and rustic furniture that managed to look both authentic and suspiciously pristine—just like Elias's attire.

Olive set her backpack on the bed and pulled out her cell phone to check for service. She had two bars now—better than she'd expected for a mountain location, but not enough to rely on if things went south.

She checked her texts and call log. Rex hadn't tried to reach her again.

Maybe he hadn't had anything urgent to share.

As she stood in the center of the room, Jason's image fluttered through her mind. He should be arriving any time now.

The kiss the two of them had shared a few months ago had awakened feelings Olive had thought were safely buried. But the unanswered questions about Jason's father's possible connection to her family's murder still hung between them like a wall of glass—transparent enough to see through, but solid enough to prevent real intimacy.

Focus on the case, she reminded herself. A missing concert organizer. Chloe's cryptic message about trees watching. An abandoned mining town that somehow figured into whatever was happening here.

The woman could have fled on her own or had an accident that was being covered up. Perhaps she'd had a conflict with someone who'd done something to her, or it was possible one of her father's enemies had done something.

Personal complications would have to wait. She had too much to uncover about Chloe first.

Olive locked her laptop in the room's safe,

checked that her backup phone was hidden in her jacket's inner pocket, and headed back downstairs.

She had work to do and, in her experience, the first twenty-four hours of an investigation were crucial for gathering intelligence before people realized they were being studied.

The main floor of the lodge had filled with more guests during Olive's brief absence.

She'd done her research and knew several key guests who'd be at the festival.

The first was influencer Maya Riggs, who'd been talking about the event online for the past month. She was a cute blonde who loved attention.

Another was Connor Walsh, a music videographer who'd been hired to document the event. The man, in his early thirties, looked too handsome with his fit build and thick, dark hair to be behind the camera.

Dr. Z was also here. He was one of the financiers who'd donated to the event. He'd made his money as a venture capitalist, but he was a closet rockabilly music fan. He was in his early forties and looked more like an office guy. Plus, she wasn't sure why people called him Dr. Z.

There were others too. Key people she'd identified before coming.

Would she see any of them here at the lodge?

Olive strolled between guests, calling out a few hellos as she made her way toward the far wall, where dozens of framed photographs documented the lodge's history.

She paused, hoping to listen in to any nearby conversations. As she lingered, she glanced at the photos. There were pictures of smiling guests posed with impressive fish catches, successful hunting parties, and scenic hiking expeditions. Together they created a visual testament to Pine Ridge Lodge's reputation as an outdoor paradise.

She moved slowly along the wall, scanning all the pictures. The photos spanned at least twenty years, showing the gradual evolution of outdoor fashion and the lodge's increasing popularity.

Then she stopped.

Her breath caught as she stared at a photograph tucked among the others—a group shot of what appeared to be a corporate retreat. The caption read "Northwoods Investment Group Annual Planning Session, 2003."

In the back row, partially obscured by shadow, stood a man who was unmistakably familiar.

In fact, he looked exactly like . . . her father.

CHAPTER 6

"Olive."

The familiar voice behind her made her heart flutter despite everything.

She turned to find Jason.

Jason with his short, dark hair. His square jaw. His broad shoulders and muscular arms.

Jason who'd gone from a small-town football player to an Army Ranger, becoming all man in the process.

Her throat still went dry at the sight of him.

Even after all these months that had passed since they reconnected, his presence still affected her in ways she tried to ignore.

"You're here." She prayed her voice sounded steadier than it felt.

"Made good time on the road." He paused. "You have any problems getting here?"

She remembered the gas station and shuddered. She didn't want to bring that up. Not yet.

Besides, it wouldn't add anything to their investigation.

"It was fine," she finally answered.

Jason's gaze moved past her to the wall of photographs, and his expression changed. "Wait. Is that . . . ?"

She licked her lips. "It looks like my dad, doesn't it?"

He stepped closer, close enough that she could smell his familiar woodsy cologne and feel the warmth radiating from his body.

Her heart pounded harder. Jason was the only man she'd ever loved.

Being around him right now was downright painful—yet thrilling at the same time. She wanted both to run and to draw closer.

"The resemblance is uncanny," he murmured, squinting as he studied the photo. "Has he ever—?"

"I have no idea," Olive finished, her voice barely above a whisper. "I don't know what he would have been doing here twenty-some years ago. But you know as well as I do that he never went anywhere without a reason."

Jason's jaw tightened as he gave a single, deliberate nod.

They'd both learned enough about her father's cons to know that every location, every interaction, every seemingly random encounter had been carefully planned.

Her father had been brilliant. But, by all appearances, he'd used that brilliance for selfish gain instead of good. Though he'd claimed to work for the government, he'd secretly cheated good people out of money . . . even though Olive still wasn't sure what he'd ultimately done with all that wealth he'd stolen.

She certainly hadn't seen any of it—not that she would keep it if she did.

But that was just one more mystery surrounding her past.

"This can't be a coincidence." He rubbed his jaw as he shook his head. "Us being here, this case—"

"Mr. and Mrs. Jones!"

They turned to find Elias approaching with that same perfectly calibrated smile. Something in his eyes had sharpened, however.

"Perfect timing," Elias continued, not missing a beat. "I was just about to gather everyone for our evening meeting. We like to brief our guests on safety protocols while here in the mountains in addition to providing some information on scheduling for Grayfall."

Olive wanted to ask him about the photograph, about whether he knew anything about the Northwoods Investment Group.

But something in Elias's demeanor warned her to wait. To observe. To gather more information before showing her hand.

"I'm ready to dive in," she said instead.

"Excellent. If you'll just follow me out to the—"

Before he could finish, a scream shattered the air.

It appeared they didn't have to look for trouble. Trouble was already here.

The raw, terrified scream echoed from somewhere outside the building.

Every conversation in the main room stopped abruptly, replaced by a silence so complete that Olive could hear her own heartbeat.

Then chaos erupted as guests rushed toward the windows, voices overlapping in concerned murmurs.

"Stay inside," Elias barked, all pretense of hospitality abandoned. "Everyone stay inside until we know what's happening."

There was no way Olive was staying inside.

Instead, she rushed across the lobby and pushed

herself through the lodge's front doors. Jason stayed close behind her.

In the parking lot, a young woman with perfectly styled blonde hair stood beside a bright yellow Jeep Wrangler, her phone held high as if she'd been filming herself when something interrupted her.

She wore trendy hiking gear that looked like it had been purchased specifically for social media content, and her expression showed genuine shock.

"You guys, it just—it literally just fell right onto my windshield!" Influencer Maya Riggs stammered as other guests gathered around. Her voice carried the breathless urgency of someone used to narrating her life for an audience. "I was doing a sunset story for my followers, and this thing just dropped out of nowhere!"

Olive moved closer to get a better look.

A large crow lay across the Jeep's hood, its black feathers stark against the white paint. Even from several feet away, she could see that its neck was bent at an unnatural angle.

"Now, now, Maya." Elias's voice sounded smooth and reassuring as he appeared beside the distressed influencer. "I know it's startling, but birds do occasionally fly into windows. The poor thing probably just got disoriented in the changing light."

Olive couldn't help but think that something about his explanation sounded rehearsed.

"But it didn't fly into anything," Maya protested, lowering her phone. "It just . . . fell. Like someone dropped it." She glanced around nervously. "This is so not the vibe I was going for in my festival preview content."

"There are natural occurrences to consider also," Elias added. "Birds sometimes suffer heart attacks, especially during seasonal migration patterns."

Olive caught Jason's eye and saw her own skepticism reflected in his gaze. Birds didn't typically fall out of clear skies onto parked cars.

Connor Walsh, the videographer, stepped closer. "That's definitely not like any normal bird behavior I've ever seen."

"Why don't we all head inside for dinner? We can do the briefing there." Elias guided Maya away from her vehicle. "I'll have Leif, my assistant, take care of this little situation, and by morning everything will be back to normal."

As the group reluctantly moved back toward the lodge, Olive lingered to study the scene. The crow's eyes were still open, reflecting the porch lights like black glass. Something about the bird's placement nagged at her.

The crow's positioning looked almost . . . deliberate. It was too centered on the hood, almost as if it had been precisely positioned.

Was Maya lying about it dropping out of the sky?

Or was Olive reading too much into this?

"Coming?" Jason appeared at her elbow, his voice low.

"Yeah." Olive forced herself to look away from the dead bird. "Just thinking about what kind of person stages something like that."

"You think it was staged?"

"Don't you?"

His nod was almost imperceptible. "It seems the most likely scenario. But why would she do that?"

"For attention," Olive suggested. "Or as a distraction from something else."

"You think Maya might actually be involved in this?"

"I'm saying, we should keep an open mind. At this point, anything is possible."

CHAPTER 7

Back inside the lodge, Elias was already directing guests toward the dining room, his hospitality mask firmly back in place.

Olive made mental notes of everyone present: Dr. Z checking his phone—probably the stock market, Maya being consoled by Connor Walsh as he showed her photos on his camera, and several other guests whose stories she hadn't heard yet.

What she didn't see was any sign of Tevin.

Her colleague should have arrived by now, using his cover as a podcaster documenting underground festival scenes for his music website, "Off the Beaten Track." The plan was for Olive and Jason to maintain their distance from Tevin. They needed to appear as if they didn't know him so they could gather more intelligence.

Speaking of which . . . she was wasting valuable time right now.

She needed to explore more of this lodge. She wanted to get a feel for the layout—just in case. She had no proof Chloe had ever been there. And though Elias was allowing people to stay here and others to simply park here before heading to Grayfall, she was unsure about his exact involvement in things.

"Excuse me," Olive murmured to Jason. "I'm going to run to the restroom."

Code: I need to investigate something.

"Take your time," he told her.

She headed toward the restrooms, located down a narrow hallway away from the lobby area. But as she approached the door leading to the ladies' room, voices from somewhere nearby made her pause.

"I can't keep doing this," a man muttered. "People are starting to ask questions."

"Questions are fine. Questions keep them distracted."

The voices came from outside, probably near a service entrance or loading dock.

Olive pressed closer to the wall, straining to hear more.

"Three people, Leif. Three. How long before someone connects—"

"They won't. As long as we stick to the plan, they won't."

Leif. Elias's assistant. Was he talking to Elias?

"But if some of these people start poking around Grayfall—"

"They won't get the chance. But keep your eyes on them. Especially that husband and wife who just arrived. There's something about them I don't trust."

Ice formed in Olive's veins.

They were talking about her and Jason. She was certain of it.

Was her cover already blown? She prayed that wasn't the case.

Olive edged closer to what she realized was a service door. She needed to hear more of that conversation. Needed to see who Leif was speaking with.

Before she could eavesdrop anymore, a footstep sounded behind her. Then, "Oh! I'm sorry, I didn't see you there."

Olive spun around to find a woman in her thirties wearing a lodge polo shirt and carrying a clipboard. The name embroidered on her shirt read "Rita—Guest Services."

"I was just looking for the restroom." Olive hoped her voice sounded casual despite her racing heart.

"Just around the corner there." Rita pointed helpfully. "Are you enjoying your stay so far? I know today's been a bit . . . eventful."

"It's been interesting, for sure." Olive glanced toward the service door, but the voices had stopped. Disappointment pressed on her. "I'm looking forward to the music festival tomorrow."

"Oh, I just know you're going to have a great time. Keep in mind that the hike to the venue can be quite challenging, especially if you're not used to mountain terrain." Rita's smile was friendly, but something in her eyes felt calculating. "Mr. Mercer always recommends staying with the guided groups for safety."

Before Olive could respond, the lodge's front door opened, and she caught sight of a familiar figure entering the main area.

Tevin. Relief filled her.

He'd finally arrived, his worn messenger bag and vintage band T-shirt perfectly selling his cover as an indie music podcaster. A few festival wristbands from previous events decorated his wrist, and he carried the slightly rumpled appearance of someone who spent more time in dive venues than corporate offices.

Every instinct told Olive to go to him, to share what she'd just overheard, to coordinate their next moves. But Olive felt Rita watching her, and she sensed others in the main room taking notice of the new arrival also.

"Well, I should run to the bathroom." Olive offered a quick smile. "Thank you for the directions —and the advice."

Rita smiled back, though the action didn't reach her eyes. "Of course. And remember—stick to the marked trails. We wouldn't want anything to happen to you."

On the surface, the words sounded like friendly advice.

But the way Rita said them felt unmistakably like a threat.

There appeared to be a lot of that going on around here.

CHAPTER 8

Back in the dining room, Olive found Jason saving her a seat at one of the long communal tables.

The lodge's dining area continued the rustic theme with exposed beam ceilings and vintage mining tools displayed on the walls. Oil lanterns provided ambient lighting that created dancing shadows in every corner.

Elias stood at the front of the room, a stein of beer in hand, commanding attention with the ease of a natural performer. "For those who are new to our little corner of West Virginia, you're staying in what was once the heart of coal country. These mountains have been home to miners and their families for over a century, and the history runs as deep as the mine-shafts themselves."

Tevin had found a spot at a table across the room, his attention apparently focused on Elias's presentation while he ate. He gave no sign of recognizing Olive, but she noticed how his gaze kept moving.

"Now, tomorrow you all will be utilizing our trail system to get to the music festival," Elias continued. "I can't stress enough the importance of staying on marked paths. These mountains can be unforgiving to those who venture off the beaten track."

"What about the missing people?" Maya spoke up, her earlier composure restored but her voice still carrying that breathless quality of someone used to dramatic storytelling. "I mean, I've been researching this area for my content, and there have been some seriously sketchy disappearances around here. Will we be safe out there?"

Elias's smile never wavered. "Those unfortunate incidents involved people who ignored safety protocols. Some ventured into areas where mountain locals don't take kindly to strangers on their property. The people around here value their privacy—and they protect it."

The way he said "mountain locals" carried a dismissive undertone that made Olive's jaw clench. It also made it clear he wasn't from this area. But she already knew that.

She'd researched the man before coming and

knew he was from Maryland, where he'd managed a successful hotel before buying this lodge.

"Are you talking about the families who've lived in these mountains for generations?" Connor lowered his camera from where he'd been videoing the room. "Because in my experience covering festivals in rural areas, most locals are incredibly welcoming. They're usually excited about the economic boost."

"Most are, yes," Elias agreed. "But isolation can breed . . . suspicion. And some areas around Grayfall in particular have residents who prefer to remain . . . shall we say—undisturbed."

"You make them sound feral," Maya noted, an eyebrow quirked. "You know, like you hear creepy stories about online. I've heard them called Dark Watchers."

Elias neither confirmed nor denied her statement.

The tension in the room was palpable.

As if desperate to move on, Elias cleared his throat and gestured toward a large topographical map mounted on the wall. "These mountains are full of natural wonders—limestone caves that stretch for miles, waterfalls hidden in remote gorges, wildlife that exists nowhere else in the state. Some say these hills are even home to creatures of legend."

Someone laughed nervously. "You mean like Bigfoot?"

"West Virginia has its own legends," Elias said with a grin. "Ever heard of the Mothman? Red eyes, massive wings, appears before disasters? Point Pleasant isn't that far from here, and some say the creature never left the area."

More nervous laughter rippled through the room, but Olive wasn't amused. She'd encountered enough real monsters in human form to know that the supernatural was usually a convenient way to explain away very human crimes.

"The point is, these mountains demand respect," Elias continued. "Stay on the trails, travel in groups, and always let someone know your planned route. Do that, and you'll have an incredible festival experience. Speaking of which, I should mention that some of the artists will be arriving by helicopter due to the remote location, so don't be alarmed if you hear aircraft tomorrow—it's all part of bringing you this unique musical experience."

As conversations resumed around the individual tables, Olive felt a flutter of nerves.

Somewhere in the abandoned mining town of Grayfall, answers waited.

The question was: What would others do to keep them from finding them?

Dinner had been surprisingly good—locally sourced trout with wild mushrooms, fresh bread that steamed when broken open, and a blackberry cobbler that tasted like someone's grandmother had made it with love and butter. Under different circumstances, Olive might have actually enjoyed the meal.

Instead, she found herself picking at her food while her mind wandered to the photograph she'd seen on the wall. Her father, standing in the back row of that corporate retreat photo like he belonged there. Like he was just another businessman enjoying a weekend in the mountains.

But James Sterling, if that had even been his real name—Olive still wasn't sure—never did anything without an ulterior motive. Every smile had been calculated, every conversation a chess move in some larger game she'd never fully understood.

What were you really doing here, Dad? What kind of scheme were you involved in?

She could picture him at this very table, charming the other guests with stories that sounded true but probably weren't. He'd always been good at making others feel like they were the most interesting person in the room while quietly memorizing their weaknesses, their desires, their bank account numbers.

For years, Olive had believed his cover story about working for the government. The excuse had explained the constant moves, the new identities, the way he always seemed to know things he shouldn't.

But after his death—after her entire family's murder—she'd learned the truth about who he really was.

A con man. A thief. A man who destroyed lives for profit.

And now she was sitting in a place where he'd apparently conducted business twenty-plus years ago.

"—So we'll see everyone bright and early to head to the festival." Elias's voice cut through her dark thoughts. "Please remember our safety protocols. And as always, if you see anything unusual in the woods, don't investigate on your own. Report it to lodge staff immediately."

The way he emphasized "anything unusual" made Olive's skin crawl. What exactly were they expecting people to see out there?

Conversations resumed as guests began pushing back from their tables, some heading toward the lobby's fireplace for nightcaps while others made their way toward the stairs and their rooms.

Olive noticed that Dr. Z was adding something on his calculator while Conner clutched his camera like it contained state secrets. Maya was already pulling out her phone, probably planning her next social media post despite the spotty service.

"Ready to head up?" Jason's voice sounded carefully neutral.

Olive nodded, acutely aware of the other guests who might be watching their interactions. She needed to stick to her cover story.

She'd perfected the art of taking on new personas when she'd been growing up. That made this undercover career perfect for her.

"I'm exhausted," she murmured. "It's been a long day. But I can't wait to see what tomorrow brings. You know what they say . . ."

"What's that?"

"Down in the holler where the shadows grow long, there's whispers in the wind of something gone wrong. So listen real close to what the old folks say, some places are meant to stay hidden away."

The lyrics felt hollow in her mouth, but they fit the situation perfectly.

She and Jason were just another couple about to walk into whatever trap was waiting for them in Grayfall.

CHAPTER 9

Olive and Jason made their way upstairs in comfortable silence. But the moment Jason closed their room door behind them, awkwardness hit like a physical force.

One bed.

King-sized, covered in a handmade quilt, sitting there like an elephant in a room that suddenly felt much smaller than it had a few hours ago.

They had a lot to talk about, and their discussion made more sense here than it did behind the flimsy fabric walls of the tent they'd share later.

Olive had done the footwork for this investigation since Jason had been on another assignment. She needed to share what she'd learned.

Plus, talking about the case was much more appealing than talking about their relationship.

"We shouldn't waste any more time." She grabbed the notes she'd brought with her from her bag. "I need to catch you up."

The two of them sat on the floor, their backs against the bed, and made themselves comfortable. She started by sharing with him the conversation she'd overheard Elias having.

She thought about telling him about the incident at the gas station, but she decided not to. That confrontation shouldn't affect their investigation.

Next, Olive grabbed Chloe's picture. She placed it in front of them.

In the lamplight, the missing woman's photograph seemed to watch them—blonde hair perfectly styled, expensive jewelry catching the camera flash, a confident smile that suggested she'd never encountered a problem that couldn't be solved with money or connections.

"Chloe Marie Kingston, twenty-four years old," Olive read from the file. "Graduated from Vassar with a degree in art history that she's never used. No employment history before Grayfall except for a brief stint at her father's company that lasted exactly six weeks."

"Let me guess." Jason read through a printout of her social media posts. "She found the corporate world 'stifling' and decided to 'find herself' through travel."

"Bingo." Olive flipped through printed Instagram posts that told the story of a young woman who'd spent the last three years jet-setting across the globe. Bali yoga retreats, safari adventures in Kenya, wine tours through Tuscany—all funded by Daddy's tech fortune. "According to her father, she never stayed anywhere longer than a few months. She was always restless, always looking for the next adventure."

The posts painted a picture of someone who'd never learned to appreciate what she had because she'd never had to work for any of it. Captions full of pseudo-philosophical musings about "authentic experiences" and "connecting with my true self," interspersed with complaints about hotel service and flight delays.

"So why did she decide to finally get a job in West Virginia?" Jason asked.

"Apparently, she loves rockabilly music, as it's called. The man who's organizing the festival—Brad Kellerman—followed her online and asked for her help. I guess she decided to give it a shot, thinking the change would be good for her. Plus, she had a good circle of influence. I'm sure it was a win-win."

"Sounds like it."

"Here's the interesting part." Olive pointed to more printed social media posts. "Two weeks before Chloe came to West Virginia, she went through a very public breakup with some British aristocrat named Tristan Pembroke. He was apparently cheating on her with her best friend."

"Ouch." Jason shook his head. "Where is this Tristan guy now?"

"I'm not sure. Tevin's working on finding out."

"He could be involved."

Olive had thought the same thing. "He's definitely someone to keep in mind."

Tristan was one of her top suspects right now . . . Tristan and Brad Kellerman.

However, Olive had no idea if Tristan was even on this side of the ocean. She hadn't been able to track him down.

In fact, it appeared he had disappeared also.

Olive continued studying the timeline. "After Chloe and Tristan's breakup is when the tone of her social media posts changed."

Chloe's earlier posts had been bright and optimistic, full of heart emojis and gratitude hashtags. But after the breakup, Chloe's captions became darker, more introspective. References to feeling "betrayed by everyone I trusted" and needing to "disappear from the fake people in my life" and "found a new opportunity."

"Then there's this." Jason pointed to a post from

three days before her disappearance. "Going off-grid for a while. Don't look for me. Sometimes you have to lose yourself to find yourself. #nocontact #digitaldetox #newbeginnings."

"Which is why the local police didn't take her disappearance seriously," Olive said. "They assumed she was having a quarter-life crisis and vanished voluntarily."

"Except for this." Jason picked up a sheet with her final text message, the one that had prompted her father to hire Aegis.

There's more to Grayfall than you think. The trees are watching.

Olive stared at the words that had seemed cryptic before. But now, after hearing Elias's presentation about mountain folklore and local legends, the message felt even more ominous.

"What do you think she meant by 'There's more to Grayfall than you think'?" Olive sucked on her bottom lip as she thought through the possibilities.

"Could be anything. A drug operation. Human trafficking. Maybe she had an argument with a colleague or made someone mad." Jason rubbed a hand over his eyes, fatigue evident in his voice. "Or it could be the ramblings of someone having a psychological breakdown after her world fell apart."

She studied his face a moment, reading him like a book. "You don't believe that any more than I do."

"No," he admitted. "I don't. Three people missing. We can't ignore that."

Olive gathered the papers back into their file, her mind already working through the logistics for this investigation. "We need to talk to more people, find out what they might know."

"Agreed. But we'll need to be careful. We have no idea what's going on here or how deeply it runs."

She swallowed hard. No, they didn't.

But a bad feeling swirled in her gut concerning this entire investigation . . . a feeling she hadn't felt in a long, long time.

CHAPTER 10

As their discussion about the case wound down, familiar tension settled between Olive's shoulders.

The tension of her and Jason's relationship, their past, of unspoken conversations.

She busied herself putting away her notes, though she felt Jason's presence beside her like heat from a fire.

This cover required intimacy they couldn't fake, in a room designed for couples who actually wanted to share space.

She leaned back against the bed, hating how nervous she felt. She prided herself on being calm, cool, and collected. "So, how was your last assignment?"

Jason leaned back also and shrugged. "I managed

to track down the father. He wasn't dead. He simply didn't want to be a dad anymore and wanted instead to start fresh somewhere else."

"Some people . . ."

He glanced at her and nodded. "Yes, some people."

Another moment of awkward silence stretched between them.

"Olive, I know you've been avoiding me," Jason finally started, the hard lines on his face softening some. "What I'm not sure about is why. Are you upset I'm working for Aegis? They approached me, just for the record."

"I'm not upset. I think you're a good fit." Her words were sincere.

"Ever since I was hired, you've sounded stiff and distracted whenever we talk on the phone. Something is obviously going on."

She wished she could deny his words, but she couldn't. Instead of answering directly, she said, "I thought you liked working for Conglomerate."

"I did, but I was ready for a change. Ready to be in the field instead of supervising security." His gaze lingered on her.

She couldn't deny that Jason made a great Aegis agent. But working with him complicated everything. *Everything.*

Rex had brought it up once. *I take it you'll be able to keep your professional boundaries in place?*

Of course, Olive had said yes. What choice did she have if she wanted to keep her job? But Jason being her colleague threw her into an emotional tailspin.

She glanced at him now. Should she even open up this can of worms about why she was keeping her distance? It could compromise her ability to fully focus on the case right now.

And that wasn't fair to Chloe or her family. They deserved her full attention.

"I just have a lot on my mind," she finally told him. "It's not personal."

He stared at her another moment before slowly nodding. "Okay then. Maybe we can talk things through when you're ready. Because, Olive, . . . I know exactly what I want."

"And what's that?" As soon as she asked the question, she realized her mistake.

"You." The word sounded low, quiet—and intimate.

Her cheeks warmed.

At once, she remembered their last kiss. She'd love more than anything to recreate it.

But Jason didn't know the things she knew—at least, to her knowledge he didn't know.

She needed to figure out how to navigate this situation. Too much was on the line not to.

CHAPTER 11

"I'll take the floor," Jason finally said after seeming to realize Olive wasn't going to respond to his statement about only wanting her.

"Are you sure? I can—"

But Jason had already risen. He began to pull extra blankets from the closet, his movements efficient but tense. The sight of him preparing to sleep on hardwood floors sent an unexpected pang through her chest.

It wouldn't be comfortable, and she was just as capable of sleeping on the floor.

"Jason, you don't have to—"

"It's fine." He didn't look at her as he arranged the blankets into a makeshift bed near the window. "I've slept in worse places."

Silence stretched between them, filled with all the words they weren't saying.

Words about the kiss they'd shared that had awakened feelings Olive thought were safely buried. About the investigation into his father's business dealings that had revealed troubling connections to her family. About the way her pulse still quickened when Jason was close, despite all the rational reasons she had to keep her distance.

Their eyes met across the room, and for a moment the careful professional masks they wore slipped away.

Olive saw in his gaze the same confusion she felt —the push and pull of attraction and suspicion, trust and fear, the past and an uncertain future.

She wanted to cross the room, to close the distance between them and deal with the consequences later. But she also wanted to demand answers about his father, about the house, about whether the man she was falling for could somehow be connected to the worst tragedy of her life.

"Tomorrow we start looking for answers about Chloe. And maybe . . ." She hesitated, then decided to voice the thought that had been haunting her since she'd seen the photograph. "Maybe if I have any free time, I'll figure out what my father was doing here more than twenty years ago."

"Olive." Jason's voice was soft, careful. "Whatever we discover about the past, whatever connections we uncover—it doesn't change who you are now."

Her throat tightened with emotion.

She wanted to believe him. But she wasn't sure she did.

Her father's blood ran through her. Sometimes she caught herself acting like him even.

That was the last thing she wanted.

Outside their window, the mountain forest stretched endlessly into darkness, hiding secrets.

But the main question in her mind was whether the man about to sleep three feet away from her was someone she could trust with her heart . . . or if he was just another beautiful lie in a life that had been built on too many of them already.

"We should get some sleep," Olive finally said, ready to turn off her emotions.

Jason nodded, already settling onto his bedroll. "Yeah. Long day tomorrow."

She changed in the bathroom, emerging in pajama pants and an oversized T-shirt that suddenly felt inadequate given their sleeping arrangements. Jason had turned off the main lights, leaving only the small bedside lamp casting warm shadows across the room.

Before climbing into bed, she cracked the second-story window just an inch. It had cooled off outside, and some fresh air sounded nice.

"Good night," she said softly.

"Good night, Olive."

She slid under the covers, hyperaware of every sound Jason made as he settled on the hardwood floor. The rustle of blankets, the quiet sigh as he found a comfortable position, the steady rhythm of his breathing that gradually slowed as he drifted toward sleep.

This was ridiculous. She was a trained investigator who had faced down armed criminals and international conspiracies. She should be able to handle sharing a room with a colleague without her heart racing like a lovesick teenager's.

But lying there in the darkness, listening to Jason breathe just feet away from her, all she could think about was the kiss they'd shared. The way his hands had felt in her hair, the warmth of his body pressed against hers, the moment when she'd felt sixteen and in love again.

She'd been so sure that night that they were moving toward something real, something worth the risk. She'd kept herself at a distance from people—from romance—for so long. But Jason had reawakened something in her. Made her wonder if being alone wasn't her only option.

Then she'd discovered the connection between his father and her family's house, and everything had become complicated again. Apparently, a shell company now owned her old home in Oasis, Texas. With the help of Tevin, Olive had done some digging and discovered that Lloyd Stewart—Jason's father—was a part of that very shell company.

What if Jason is innocent? The thought whispered through her mind like a prayer. *What if his father's business dealings had nothing to do with what happened to my family?*

But what if they did?

Olive certainly didn't want people judging her for her father's actions. So was it really fair that she was doing it to Jason?

No, it wasn't.

However, a lot was at stake here, and she had to be careful. She needed to find some answers before she made any decisions.

She couldn't handle being conned by anyone—especially not someone she cared about. It would devastate her.

A sound outside made her freeze. Muffled but agitated voices came from the woods behind the lodge.

Olive quietly slipped from the bed and padded to

the window. The moon provided just enough light to make out shapes moving in the shadows at the edge of the forest.

Two figures stood about fifty yards from the lodge. One she recognized immediately as Elias Mercer. His posture appeared rigid with anger or maybe frustration.

The other was harder to make out. He was shorter, scrawnier. Leif maybe.

Their voices carried on the still night air, though most of the words were lost.

But then Elias's voice rose, clear and sharp with panic. "Some things are out of my control. You're asking too much!"

Olive remained at the window, her breath fogging the glass as she strained to see into the darkness.

Elias and the other man had walked toward the maintenance shed behind the lodge and vanished.

The part of their conversation she'd overheard played on repeat in her mind—the urgency in Elias's voice, the way he'd said "some things are out of my control" like he was announcing the arrival of some dreaded inevitability.

What kind of place is this?

She remembered what Elias had said about the

waterfalls and caves in this area. There appeared to be innumerous places for crimes to happen.

For bodies to be hidden.

Olive had investigated many things, but something about this case felt different. More personal. More dangerous in ways she couldn't articulate.

She was about to step away from the window when more movement in her peripheral vision made her freeze.

A figure stood deep in the woods, barely visible among the shadows cast by overlapping pine branches. It was too dark to make out any of his features, but if Olive had to guess, the man was wearing a dark hooded sweatshirt. She had only the light of an almost-full moon to illuminate the area.

Her heart slammed against her ribs as she watched. The figure wasn't hiding. He wasn't trying to blend into the forest or move stealthily through the undergrowth.

He was simply standing there, watching the lodge.

How long had the man been there? Had he witnessed Elias's conversation with the other man? Was he connected to whatever had happened to Chloe, or was he another variable in an already complicated equation?

"Olive?" Jason's voice was barely a whisper behind her. "What is it?"

She didn't dare look away from the window, afraid that any movement might alert the watcher to the fact that he'd been spotted.

"Someone is out there," she murmured. "In the trees. He's watching the lodge."

The soft rustle of Jason rising from his bed sounded, then his quiet footsteps as he crossed the room to join her at the window.

"Where?" His voice was right beside her ear now, close enough that she could feel the warmth of his breath against her neck, that she could smell his woodsy cologne.

More than anything, she wanted to turn. To step toward him. To get lost in his kisses.

Her pulse pounded harder.

But she couldn't allow herself to go there.

"Right there, by that cluster of—" Olive blinked, the words dying in her throat.

The woods were now empty.

In her brief moment of distraction, the man had disappeared.

Now she only saw shadows and pine branches swaying gently in the mountain breeze, creating patterns that could trick the eye into seeing movement where none existed.

Jason squinted. "I don't see anyone."

Olive pressed closer to the glass, scanning every

shadow, every gap between trees where a person could hide.

But there was nothing.

No hooded figure. No sign anyone had ever been standing there at all.

Her hands fisted at her sides.

"He was right there," she insisted, though doubt had crept into her voice. "I saw him clearly. He was watching the lodge."

Jason's hand covered her shoulder, warm and reassuring. "These mountains can play tricks on your eyes, especially at night. Shadows, wind through the trees—"

"I know what I saw." But even as she said the words, Olive found herself questioning her own perception.

The stress of the case, the unsettling dinner conversation, the awkwardness of their sleeping arrangements—maybe her mind was creating threats where none existed.

But the feeling of being watched and of being studied by unseen eyes lingered like a chill that had seeped into her bones.

The two of them stood at the window for several more minutes, both scanning the darkness for any sign of movement.

The forest remained still, innocent, revealing nothing of its secrets.

"We should get some sleep," Jason finally said.

Olive nodded reluctantly, though every instinct screamed at her to keep watching, to stay alert for whatever was lurking in the darkness beyond the glass.

She pulled the curtains closed and returned to bed, but sleep felt impossible.

She lay in the darkness listening to Jason settle back onto his blankets, acutely aware of every sound from outside—the whisper of wind through pine needles, the distant hoot of an owl, the creak of tree branches that could be nature settling or could be something else entirely.

The trees are watching.

Chloe Kingston's final message took on new meaning as Olive stared at the ceiling.

What if her message hadn't been the ramblings of a depressed young woman having a breakdown? What if it had been a literal warning about the dangers hidden in these woods?

Now she and Jason were planning to walk directly into that same wilderness, following trails that might lead them to answers—or might lead them to become victim numbers four and five.

The bad feeling in Olive's gut intensified as she finally drifted toward an uneasy sleep filled with dreams of hooded figures and trees with eyes and voices in the darkness whispering about things that were happening again.

CHAPTER 12

ELEVEN YEARS AGO, BLUE RIDGE MOUNTAINS, GEORGIA

Olive's family had been hiking for two hours on a well-traveled trail that wound up the mountain.

The late morning air carried the earthy scent of decomposing leaves and the clean smell of granite warmed by early sunlight. Olive's boots crunched softly on the gravel path as she adjusted her pack straps, her legs already feeling the burn from the steady uphill climb.

They'd passed several people since they started, which made her feel a little better.

At least they weren't out here alone.

When they reached a scenic overlook, Dad paused. Another family was there taking photographs.

A well-dressed couple with expensive camera

equipment was positioning their teenage son in front of the vista. Their voices carried the cadence of people accustomed to having their vacation plans accommodate any whim.

The woman wore designer hiking boots while her husband sported a high-tech outdoor jacket that made subtle statements about disposable income. Their son shifted awkwardly as they directed his poses, clearly more interested in the handheld gaming device tucked into his jacket pocket than the stunning mountain panorama behind him.

"Beautiful morning for treasure hunting, isn't it?" Dad called out, his voice carrying that warm, engaging tone that could make strangers feel like old friends within minutes.

The woman lowered her camera—a professional-grade Canon that gleamed silver and black in the sunlight—and turned toward them with the polite but slightly guarded smile of someone interrupted during a private family moment.

"Treasure hunting?" she asked.

The familiar flutter of anxiety captured Olive's stomach. Here it comes, she thought as she watched her father's face transform into what she'd learned to recognize as his "showtime" expression.

She knew it well. Knew the way his eyes slightly widened. The way his smile became more animated.

The subtle shift in his posture that made him appear both trustworthy and knowledgeable.

"Family tradition." Dad gestured to his brood of excited children with the kind of paternal pride that looked absolutely genuine.

The twins bounced on their toes beside him, their matching purple backpacks and gap-toothed grins making them look like poster children for wholesome family adventures.

"We're following an old Civil War-era treasure map," he continued. "Allegedly, there's buried gold somewhere in these mountains."

"Really? That's fascinating." The man stepped closer and extended his hand. "We're the Hendersons, from Atlanta. This is our son Michael's sixteenth birthday celebration."

"James Sterling." Dad grasped the offered hand with the kind of firm, confident grip that suggested reliability and competence. "What a perfect way to celebrate a birthday. History coming alive in these beautiful mountains."

Her father's movements became more enthusiastic as he pulled the leather portfolio from his pack.

Her mother hung back with the twins, her expression neutral as she fidgeted with the straps of Jessie's backpack, adjusting and readjusting them.

"This is incredible." Mrs. Henderson examined

the hand-drawn map, her voice filled with genuine awe. "It looks so authentic."

Dad's smile held just the right mixture of pride and humility. "Doesn't it, though? I've been planning this expedition for months. Michael, you look like a young man who appreciates history. What do you think of our treasure map?"

The teenager stepped closer, his earlier boredom evaporating. The gaming device disappeared back into his pocket as he studied the documents with growing excitement. "Is this a real-life treasure hunt? Now *that* would be a fun birthday surprise."

"Well . . ." Dad winked in a way that made him look like a favorite uncle sharing secrets. "That depends on how competent we are at solving riddles and reading the land. But I have a good feeling about today."

His voice carried such genuine warmth and confidence that even Olive, who knew better, felt a flutter of possibility.

Maybe this time would be different. Maybe this time, the treasure hunt would be real, the family adventure would be exactly what it appeared to be, and her father's stories would lead somewhere magical instead of manipulative.

She only wished she could really believe that.

But as she watched Mrs. Henderson's eyes light up with an excitement that made smart people make foolish decisions, the familiar weight of dread settled in Olive's chest like a stone.

The mountain air that had seemed so fresh and invigorating moments before now felt thin and insufficient.

It was as if the wilderness itself was holding its breath, waiting to see how this performance would unfold.

Olive couldn't help but wonder if her dad had planned this whole outing in hopes of running into this family and unleashing another one of his scams.

CHAPTER 13

PRESENT DAY

Olive woke to silence and the scent of pine.

At once, everything slammed back into her mind. The assignment. Seeing her father's picture. Jason.

Jason . . .

She looked at the floor. His makeshift bed was empty, blankets folded with military precision.

For a moment, panic fluttered in her chest.

Jason never left without telling her, and she prided herself on being a light sleeper who noticed everything.

Just then, the bathroom door opened and released a cloud of steam and the sound of running water being turned off.

Either Olive was really out last night or Jason was extremely light on his feet.

Jason emerged wearing jeans and a flannel shirt, his dark hair damp from the shower.

Her heart lurched into her throat. Even after all these years, the sight of him caught her off guard sometimes—the way his presence filled a room, the easy confidence in his movements, the fact that he looked like he belonged wherever he went.

Keep your emotions in check, she reminded herself sternly. *Professional. Distant. Safe.*

"Morning." He avoided her eyes as he packed his toiletries.

"How'd you sleep?" The question came out more stilted than Olive had intended.

"Not great." He glanced toward the window where she'd seen—or thought she'd seen—the hooded figure last night. "You?"

"Same." She sat up, pulling the covers around herself like armor. "You ready for this?"

Jason paused from packing. "I'm not sure any of us are ready for whatever we're walking into out there."

The honesty in his voice made something twist in her chest.

Olive had never been much of a hiker—her idea of outdoor recreation usually involved surveillance from the comfort of a rental car, not trudging through wilderness with a backpack.

Her father had taken her hiking exactly once,

when she was fourteen and they were living in Georgia. That had been a disaster.

The memory brought with it others she tried to avoid—conversations with Jason back in high school when they'd been young and naive and full of impossible dreams. They'd talked about getting married someday and hiking the Appalachian Trail together.

She'd been willing to give hiking another shot—but only with Jason.

They'd also talked about buying a house in the mountains and raising kids who knew how to build campfires and identify constellations.

Big plans from two teenagers who thought love could conquer anything. Those were the days before her father had woken her and the family at three a.m. and told them to pack only what mattered because they were leaving and never coming back. He forbade her from staying in touch with anyone in town, saying it was a matter of life or death.

"If not for yourself, then think of your sisters," her dad had warned her.

Olive would have done anything for Jules and Jessie.

Those conversations had taken place before Olive's heart had been broken so completely that she'd spent years learning how to keep people at a distance.

She should have known better than to get attached. But she'd gotten attached anyway.

Opening up her heart had been her biggest mistake. She couldn't go through that again.

She sat up straighter and pushed the memories aside. "We should head down for breakfast. Get a feel for who else is going on this hike."

Jason nodded. "Sounds like a plan."

She still felt the strain stretching between them, and more than anything, she wished she could erase it.

But unfortunately, erasing tension wasn't one of her superpowers.

Instead, just like so many things in her life, she would need to learn to live with it and try to make the best of things.

The dining room buzzed with electric excitement, the air thick with anticipation and caffeine-fueled energy. Olive picked at her eggs and bacon while watching everyone around her, but it was hard to concentrate over the infectious enthusiasm filling the space.

Outside the dining room windows, a steady stream of vehicles was pulling into the parking area. Subarus and Priuses with festival stickers, luxury SUVs with roof-mounted gear, even a few vintage

VW buses that looked like they'd driven straight out of Woodstock.

Groups of twenty-somethings spilled out of cars, their laughter and excited chatter floating through the windows as they unloaded hiking gear and compared their expensive festival wristbands. Several of them wore cowboy hats. A couple carried guitars in soft-carry cases.

Multiple flat-screen TVs mounted around the room played a slick promotional video on repeat, the footage so professionally shot it could have been advertising Coachella or Bonnaroo.

Aerial drone shots swept over misty mountains before cutting to intimate performance footage—artists silhouetted against dramatic lighting and crowds swaying with hands raised.

It was the kind of authentic moments that took teams of videographers to capture. The production values were stunning, with a soundtrack that made even breakfast feel epic.

The footage clearly wasn't from the Grayfall Music Fest since this was the first year it was taking place. But organizers had worked hard—and spent a lot of money—to make this.

Olive had seen it before. The video had been all over social media. And she could understand why music lovers might flock to this opportunity.

Her breath caught when she saw Chloe on the screen.

Olive exchanged a look with Jason.

Chloe? She hadn't been in the original promo video.

Somehow, this felt important.

Olive leaned closer, not wanting to miss any details.

CHAPTER 14

Chloe Kingston laughed on screen as a crowd behind her partied.

Her blonde hair caught the golden hour light as she gestured enthusiastically toward the camera, her voice carrying over the music. "Grayfall isn't just a festival—it's a transformation. We're creating something that's never been done before, where music and wilderness and human connection become one incredible experience."

The camera pulled back to show the scene behind her—dozens of beautiful people dancing and drinking, their high-end festival outfits pristine despite the supposed "wilderness" setting.

But something felt off about their enthusiasm. Their smiles were too bright, their movements too choreographed. They were more like actors who'd been directed to look like they were having the time of their lives.

The video cut to sweeping drone footage of Grayfall that made the abandoned town look mystical rather than decrepit. Strategic camera angles highlighted the dramatic mountain backdrop.

"This is about more than music," Chloe continued in a voiceover as the footage showed cloud-shrouded mountains. "It's about disconnecting from the artificial world and reconnecting with something real, something primal . . . something amazing."

The next sequence showed nighttime footage around a massive bonfire, with silhouettes dancing against the flames. The audio was a mix of acoustic guitar and laughter.

Then Chloe appeared again, this time in daylight. But her demeanor had changed subtly. The brilliant smile was still there, but it looked more forced now, and her eyes held a tension that hadn't been present in the earlier footage.

"The connection to the land, to the history of this place, to each other—it's going to be profound." There was a slight hesitation in her voice, as if she were reading words she no longer entirely believed.

The camera caught a moment when Chloe thought she was off-screen—her bright expression dropping into something more troubled as she glanced toward the mine entrance.

The footage quickly cut away, but not before Olive saw Chloe wrap her arms around herself as if suddenly cold.

The final shot returned to the party atmosphere, with Chloe back in full promotional mode. "Grayfall is going to change everything. This is where transformation happens. This is where you discover who you really are."

As the video faded to black with the festival logo, Olive couldn't shake the feeling that Chloe had discovered exactly that—and it had terrified her.

Olive's stomach clenched at the thought. She prayed the girl was okay. Prayed they'd be able to find her.

"I can't believe we're actually doing this!" squealed a girl at the next table. "The videos look insane. This is going to be the most incredible weekend ever!"

A group near the windows was already comparing the promotional footage to their expectations. "Did you see that main stage setup? This is going to be so much better than Burning Man."

The infectious excitement was palpable, making it easy to forget that three people had disappeared in these mountains. The promotional video made everything look magical and safe.

Olive wished she felt confident that was true.

Elias appeared at the front of the room, waiting for a lull in the video's soundtrack before clapping his hands for attention. "Listen up, everyone! I hope you're as excited as I am. These videos don't even do justice to what you're about to experience."

The room erupted in cheers and applause.

"The first group headed to the music festival leaves in fifteen minutes," he continued over the noise. "New groups will leave every hour until three o'clock. Do a final check of your gear, and remember—stay with the group, follow your guide's instructions, and respect the wilderness that's graciously hosting us this weekend."

More cheers filled the room, along with the scraping of chairs against hardwood as guests began gathering their belongings with renewed enthusiasm. Someone started chanting "Grayfall! Grayfall!" and others joined in.

A familiar flutter touched Olive's stomach. It was a combination of anticipation and anxiety that always preceded stepping into the unknown.

Chloe's life depended on Olive completing this assignment.

Failure wasn't an option.

But there was still one more thing she needed to do before departing.

She turned to Jason. "I need to run to the restroom. Meet you outside?"

"Sounds good." He nodded, already moving toward the door with the other festivalgoers.

Olive waited until the dining room was nearly empty.

Then she made her move.

The lodge's office was located down a short hallway behind the reception desk, its door marked with a discrete brass nameplate reading "E. Mercer—Manager." Olive had scouted out this area yesterday when she'd headed toward the bathroom.

She tried the handle, surprised—but grateful—to find it unlocked.

The space was larger than she'd expected, with windows overlooking the forest and walls lined with filing cabinets that probably contained decades of guest records, financial documents, and business correspondence. A computer sat powered down on the desk beside stacks of papers and a coffee mug with the lodge logo.

She moved quickly, scanning the visible documents for anything related to missing hikers or unusual incidents.

Most appeared to be routine business paperwork

—vendor invoices, guest registration forms, paystubs.

Then she spotted a manila folder tucked beneath a stack of brochures, partially hidden but not entirely concealed. The tab read "INCIDENT REPORTS—2025."

Olive's pulse quickened as she pulled out her phone and began photographing the contents.

Page after page of reports painted a very different picture than the one Elias had presented.

Missing person reports filed with local authorities. Search and rescue operations that had turned up nothing. Insurance claims for "presumed deceased" hikers whose bodies were never recovered.

At the back of the folder, there was a collection of newspaper clippings about the disappearances, some with handwritten notes in the margins: "Too close to Grayfall." "Hiking alone after dark." "Ignored safety protocols."

Her heart pounded harder.

There were more than three people missing. Far more than three. And most were outsiders to the area.

She kept snapping pictures. Her hands shook slightly as she captured page after page of evidence. David Brooks and Clara Holloway were just the most recent. The clippings went back several months—

hikers, campers, even a few locals who'd ventured too close to whatever was happening in Grayfall.

But Olive needed more. The photograph on the wall with her father's face haunted her, and she had to know what connection Northwoods Investment Group had to this place.

Footsteps echoed in the hallway outside, still distant but definitely approaching.

She scanned the filing cabinets, looking for anything labeled with "N" for Northwoods. Her pulse thundered in her ears as she spotted a drawer marked "N–P," and she carefully pulled it open.

The footsteps were closer now, accompanied by voices—Elias talking to someone about "getting everything in order."

Her fingers flew through the files: "News Articles," "Noise Complaints," "Night Security."

And there, near the back, a thick folder labeled "Northwoods Investment—Historical."

Working quickly, she grabbed the folder and flipped it open. The first page was a letterhead from 2003, and she could see her father's name listed as a "consulting advisor" on some kind of property development project.

The footsteps in the hall moved again, much closer now.

Voices sounded near the door.

". . . just want to grab those insurance documents before tomorrow," Elias was saying.

Olive snapped a photo of the first page, but there was so much more—maps, financial records, what looked like geological surveys.

She desperately flipped through the folder, trying to capture as much as possible. But the approaching voices made her hands shake.

The door handle rattled.

She had to get out. Now.

Olive quickly replaced the Northwoods folder, praying she'd put it back in exactly the right spot, and moved toward the window behind the desk. Her heart hammered against her ribs as she heard the key sliding into the lock.

She tugged at the window, but the old sash stuck.

No . . .

Dread filled her as she heard the lock click. She pulled harder at the window, desperation making her reckless with the noise she made.

"You really think the shuttle was sabotaged?" came a voice from the hallway. It wasn't Elias, but another voice she didn't recognize.

The window sash gave a soft groan of protest but still wouldn't budge.

"Yes, I do." Elias's voice carried a note of suspicion.

"Are you going to report it?"

"Won't do much good now."

Olive put both hands on the window frame and pulled with all her strength, not caring anymore about the sound.

The doorknob started to turn.

She tried again, her heart racing faster.

But the window wouldn't open.

What was she going to do?

CHAPTER 15

Olive gave the window one more try.

Something gave way, and the window slid up with a soft scrape.

Finally!

Olive climbed through the window frame, dropping into the flower bed outside just as voices erupted in the office.

She pressed herself against the lodge's exterior wall, her heart pounding so hard she was sure they could hear it from inside. Instead, she heard Elias say, "Can't leave this window open."

She held her breath as footsteps moved toward the window.

Would Elias peer out? Would he see her?

Instead, she heard the window squeal as it was shoved back in place.

The air left her lungs as relief filled her.

That had been close. Really close.

As she glanced at the office, she saw shadows moving inside, hands rifling through the very files she'd been photographing moments before.

She'd gotten some of the Northwoods information, but not nearly enough.

Who was the person with Elias? Did the owner have a confidante? If so, that person could be a valuable source of information.

If Olive could just get a little closer and peek inside . . .

But voices sounded in the distance. Being here was too risky.

Heart still racing, Olive hurried around the side of the building toward the front entrance where the hiking group was gathering. She spotted Jason scanning the area, probably wondering what was taking her so long.

"There you are," Elias called out as Olive approached.

He'd made it out of his office quickly.

His tone was friendly but his eyes sharp with suspicion as he observed her. "We were about to send a search party."

"Sorry." Olive prayed her voice sounded steadier than she felt. "I'm a sucker for wildlife, and I thought I saw a deer."

Elias's gaze traveled from her face to her phone, which she realized she was still clutching, then back to her eyes. "Did you?"

Did he suspect she was the one who'd been in his office?

Her muscles tensed, though she was careful not to show her apprehension.

"I did, but he ran away before I could snap a photo." She met his stare without flinching. "I'm ready to see what these mountains have to offer."

"That's what I like to hear."

As they moved toward the group of hikers, Olive prayed Elias wasn't onto her.

The incident reports she'd photographed burned in her phone's memory like evidence of crimes not yet committed. She couldn't wait to dig into them.

Whatever was happening in these mountains, the lodge staff knew more than they were saying.

She needed to find out what.

The morning air carried unmistakable anticipation as festivalgoers gathered in front of the lodge.

Olive figured there must be around a hundred people clutching coffee cups and checking their phones one last time before venturing into what the promotional materials had promised would be "the music experience of a lifetime."

Everyone had been given specific departure times. Thankfully, Olive, Jason, and Tevin were in the first group.

"Welcome, welcome!" Elias appeared in front of the crowd, his smile bright. "I hope everyone's ready for an adventure. You're about to experience something truly special—a music festival in one of the most pristine wilderness locations on the East Coast."

Cheers rippled through the crowd.

"As you know, I've partnered with the organizers of Grayfall to make this a once in a lifetime experience. This music festival will be like nothing else you've ever done."

That's exactly what scares me. Olive kept her expression neutral as the crowd cheered again, effectively getting hyped.

"Now, I'd like you to meet your guides for today's journey." Elias gestured toward three men who'd positioned themselves near him. "Max, Sorrel, and Tom will be ensuring your safety and helping you navigate the trail system."

Olive studied the so-called guides. All three were built like bouncers. They had broad shoulders, watchful eyes, and alert postures.

Max carried himself with the arrogant swagger of someone who thought intimidation was a personality trait. He kept flexing his hands and cracking his knuckles, clearly hoping someone would give him an excuse to use those muscles.

Sorrel was the opposite—wiry and nervous, constantly checking his phone with the twitchy intensity of someone monitoring multiple security feeds at once. His eyes never stopped moving, cataloging every detail around him as if he were expecting trouble from every direction. Everything about him screamed "tech surveillance."

Tom looked bored with the whole operation, leaning against a tree like someone who'd done this routine too many times to find it interesting anymore. Unlike his companions, he had the weathered look of actual mountain experience and kept checking his watch as if he had somewhere more important to be.

"Are they certified wilderness guides?" Maya asked. "My followers are always asking about safety certifications for adventure experiences."

"They're experienced outdoorsmen who know these mountains better than anyone." Elias's words almost sounded rehearsed.

Jason caught Olive's eye, his slight frown indicating he'd also noticed how these men moved like security personnel, not hospitality staff or wilderness guides.

"Now, I do have one small update about today's logistics." Elias's tone remained overly cheerful.

"Originally, we were supposed to have shuttle service to the trailhead. But the shuttle is experiencing some mechanical issues this morning. Nothing serious, but it means we'll need to start our hike from here at the lodge instead."

A collective groan sounded from several attendees.

"How much extra distance are we talking about?" A man who looked like a frat boy with his backward baseball hat and polo asked.

"Just a few extra miles." Elias offered a dismissive wave. "Five miles, maybe six. Really, it's a blessing in disguise. You'll get to see parts of these mountains that most tourists never experience."

Five or six miles on top of what was already supposed to be a challenging hike to reach the festival grounds? If they departed by ten, this hike would probably take five hours, plus they'd stop for lunch. They wouldn't get to Grayfall until close to four. The first concert was scheduled to start at eight.

It was going to be a long, long day.

Olive watched the faces around her as the reality sank in. Several people were already struggling with the weight of their packs, and they hadn't even started walking yet.

That was when all the questions erupted.

CHAPTER 16

"Will there be water stations along the extended route?" Dr. Z had a pensive look on his face as more facts unfolded.

"The trail follows several natural water sources," Max—who, based on the way he stepped out in front of the others, appeared to be in charge—answered. "Our guides will have some filters with them, just in case."

"What about emergency protocols?" Maya pressed. "What happens if someone gets injured on this extended route? My audience needs to know about safety measures—especially if you're planning on making this an annual event."

How things went today would determine this festival's future success. Certainly organizers had to realize that.

"Ma'am, these mountains have been safely traveled for generations." Max's smile didn't reach his eyes. "As long as everyone follows instructions and stays with the group, there won't be any problems."

The way he emphasized "follows instructions" made Olive's skin crawl.

She'd heard that tone before—from people who were used to ensuring compliance through intimidation rather than cooperation.

A slightly overweight twentysomething man near the back of the crowd stepped forward. "I'm starting to think maybe I should just drive back to civilization and catch the next festival. This is way more intense than what I signed up for. I didn't know I would need to have fitness training before coming here."

The response was immediate and telling.

Ticket holders weren't happy with this development. The good news was that they didn't have to carry in supplies—only their backpacks, which would probably be challenging in and of itself. Luxury accommodations had been promised. Glamping style tents. Gourmet food. Meet and greets with the artists. Intimate bonfires with guest musicians.

All three guides shifted slightly, their attention focusing on the speaker with laser precision. Max took a step closer to the young man, while Sorrel's hand moved to his belt where Olive now noticed he carried what looked like a radio.

"You've already paid for the full experience. It would be a shame to miss out on something this unique." He paused. "And besides, the window for refunds has already passed."

The young man's face paled slightly. "But I thought—"

"Trust me." Max kept his stiff stance, but his voice lightened just slightly. "Once you see what we've put together out there, you'll be glad you stayed."

"All right, everyone!" Elias clapped his hands together. "Let's get ready to go!"

But the crowd wouldn't have it. They still had more questions.

"How are the artists getting there?" someone called. "Do they also have to hike in with their things? Their instruments?"

"Were you not listening when I explained before?" Elias's cheek twitched with irritation. "As I said, most of them are coming in via helicopter."

Murmurs of dissatisfaction went around the group.

"You must understand the logistics of transporting five hundred people that way would be impossible," Elias tried to explain, a layer of sweat stretching across his forehead.

"What about ATVs?" someone else called out. "Couldn't they transport us?"

"Again, the logistics don't make sense," Elias said. "Not with so many people attending."

"And there's no way a vehicle could travel down this road?" another man asked.

"It's closed to private vehicles by order of the county," Elias continued. "Fallen trees have blocked the road, plus underbrush has grown up. We got special permission to use our shuttle to carry people part of the way."

"It seems like with all the money we've paid for the festival, you guys could have afforded to hire someone to remove the trees for the event!"

Elias's smile was still present, but his patience appeared to be fading. "Then you wouldn't have the whole experience."

"I'm here for the music and camping, not this 'whole experience' thing you keep talking about," someone complained.

Others joined in with murmured grievances.

More questions started, but he cut them off with the shake of his head.

"We're wasting valuable time here," he told everyone. "Let's get those packs adjusted and hit the trail. Adventure awaits, and Midnight Echo is on the schedule for this evening!"

As people begrudgingly began moving toward their gear, Olive feared these festivalgoers didn't fully know what they were getting themselves into.

CHAPTER 17

The trail wound through dense forest that seemed to press closer with each step. The canopy overhead filtered the morning light into shifting patterns of green and gold.

Olive adjusted her pack straps and fell into rhythm beside Jason, both of them maintaining the facade of an enthusiastic couple while their eyes constantly scanned their surroundings.

The group of a hundred had strung out over nearly a quarter mile of trail, with the strongest hikers pulling ahead and others already struggling despite the fact they'd just started the journey.

Max led the front group, his pace never varying regardless of terrain. Sorrel brought up the rear, his attention focused more on the stragglers than on the path ahead. Tom moved through the middle section like a sheepdog, subtly correcting anyone who wandered too far from the prescribed route.

Olive tried to picture this back when it was the only road leading to Grayfall.

The town, in its heyday, had boasted four thousand residents. Almost all the families in the area were connected with the mines—either working there or as the children or spouse of someone working there.

When the mines had shut down because of safety violations thirty years ago, so had the town.

Now, this road leading into town was used as a hiking path.

The remnants of bygone days, and the flood, were all around them—an occasional rusty car in the brush. Trees and debris from the flooding. And evidence of more recent "visitors"—beer cans and snack wrappers.

"How are you holding up, sweetie?" Jason asked loudly enough for nearby hikers to hear, playing his role of concerned husband.

"Things are always good when you're with me." She flashed a warm smile.

"Aww . . ." a woman nearby said. "That's so sweet."

"It's easy to be sweet when you're with someone as wonderful as Olivia."

They needed to be careful to sell their story but not overdo it. So far, so good.

She had to wonder, however, how some of these people had thought they were prepared for a wilderness music festival.

Maya was already getting a blister from her cute boots, stopping frequently to film herself with commentary like: "This hike is literally insane, you guys!"

Olive wasn't sure why she was recording everything as if it was a livestream when there was no signal to post it.

An older man who'd boasted at breakfast about all the music festivals he'd attended paused every few hundred yards to catch his breath.

Tevin maintained his position about fifty yards ahead. He'd struck up casual conversations with several other attendees, his easy manner drawing out information without seeming to pry.

Olive scanned the woods, and her breath caught.

Behind a cluster of oak trees, a shadow shifted in ways that didn't match the wind patterns.

For this entire hike, she'd been watching for signs of the wildlife Elias had mentioned, but this movement was different. It was too deliberate.

Too human.

Someone else was out here.

"We've got company." She tilted her head toward the woods.

Jason's hand found hers, the gesture appearing romantic to outside observers while actually serving as a silent signal that he'd seen something too.

Someone was paralleling their route, staying just out of sight but close enough to monitor their progress.

Her throat tightened as she waited for what might happen next.

Before she could figure out who—or what—was in the woods, a cry filled the air.

Olive jerked her gaze toward the sound to see what the commotion was about.

A woman near Tevin stumbled, her ankle turning on loose rock before she sprawled on the ground.

Everyone nearby clustered around her to make sure she was okay.

Olive glanced once more at the woods before turning back to the situation in front of her.

"It's probably just twisted," Tom said as he examined the woman's ankle. "Can you put weight on it?"

The woman tried to stand but winced. "I don't think I can make it all the way to the festival grounds."

"We'll get you some ibuprofen and wrap it up," Tom said. "You should be fine. We'll help you get there. That's what your Grayfall family is here for."

Her Grayfall family? Interesting word choice.

Everyone paused as Tom found a first-aid kit and wrapped her ankle.

As they did that, several people pulled out their lunches. They'd each been handed a paper bag before they'd left, and Olive wasn't sure what was inside.

She pulled hers out and found a sandwich with a single slice of processed cheese and a piece of lettuce.

She squinted. Was this it?

There was also a store-bought prepackaged brownie and a small bag of peanuts.

She skipped the sandwich and went right for the peanuts.

Hopefully this wasn't reflective of how the food would be for the rest of the weekend. If so, they were going to have a lot of very unhappy people at the festival.

Several others murmured their disapproval around her as they munched on their meager meal and rested against nearby logs and boulders. The break did feel nice.

However, Olive continued to keep her eyes wide open for trouble. Who had been in the woods with them? Were they still there?

When Tom was done tending to the woman with

the hurt ankle, Max turned to the rest of the group. "I know some of you are still eating, but we need to keep moving."

As the group reorganized and began walking again, Olive saw Tevin watching something in the forest. Then he looked in her direction and gave her a nod.

He knew what she knew.

They weren't alone out here.

Whoever had been in the woods wasn't gone. They were still there.

And they were watching.

CHAPTER 18

The trail began to descend, offering a small amount of relief for their weary muscles.

"Not much longer." Max's voice carried forced enthusiasm. "Just another few miles to paradise."

Just as he said the words, a man materialized from the forest like a ghost given flesh.

Olive sucked in a breath, and several people gasped or let out soft screams.

One moment the trail ahead had been empty. The next, this man stood blocking their path, emerging from what looked like a solid wall of rhododendron and mountain laurel.

No rustling branches had announced his approach, no snapping twigs. He simply appeared as if the forest itself had birthed him from its shadows.

The entire group stopped as if they'd hit an invisible wall, the cheerful chatter of the hike dying instantly.

Several people took instinctive steps backward. Maya's phone, which had been recording almost constantly, trembled in her suddenly unsteady hands.

The silence stretched, broken only by the sound of nearly a hundred people trying not to breathe too loudly.

Olive observed the man a moment. He was lean and weathered, probably in his sixties. His sun-carved features spoke of decades spent in these mountains. His clothing—faded flannel, worn denim, and boots that had seen countless miles of rough terrain—marked him as someone who belonged to this wilderness rather than someone merely visiting it.

But his eyes were what made Olive's breath catch. They held the stillness of a predatory cat, taking in every face in the group.

Behind him, just visible through gaps in the foliage, other shadows shifted. Not wind-blown branches or forest debris—movement that was more deliberate.

The Dark Watchers?

Were these the men she'd seen last night from her bedroom window? Had they sabotaged the shuttle?

Her heart pounded harder.

How many? Olive couldn't tell.

But the message was clear: This wasn't a chance encounter with a lone mountain man.

Jason moved closer as if ready to protect Olive if needed.

Funny, as of late Olive was usually the one doing the protecting. But she liked the idea of someone watching out for her—maybe she liked it a little too much.

"Y'all heading down to Grayfall?" The man's Appalachian accent was thick with generations of mountain life.

"That's right." Max's hand moved instinctively toward his radio. "Just taking some friends to see the old mining town."

The man's eyes swept the group. "Awful strange place for carryin' on like that. Been happenings down yonder in town that ain't natural-like. Things that don't belong nowhere near decent folk."

"What kind of things?" Maya's voice trembled as she asked the question.

The man's gaze fixed on her. "The kind that sends folks with a lick of sense packin' back the way they come. Everyone knows six people died in them mines. Their spirits still haunt the place, not ready to go home yet."

A chill swept over Olive.

His warning was loud and clear.

This area wasn't safe.

What Olive wasn't sure about was why.

Max stepped forward, his posture shifting into something more aggressive. "Sir, I appreciate your concern, but we're on a tight schedule. We don't want to keep people from their plans."

"Plans got a way of changin'." The man didn't back down despite Max's intimidating stance. "But some things, once they get to rollin', ain't no stoppin' 'em."

The Grayfall Guardian, Olive mused. That became this man's nickname in her mind.

As he spoke, Olive glanced into the woods. This guy had at least three friends with him. They were no longer hiding.

In fact, they all stood close, as if on standby in case things went south.

Or in case they wanted to make things go south.

Her heart pounded harder.

"Hey, hillbilly. You got any moonshine?" Frat Boy yelled from the back of the group.

Olive's muscles tightened.

A round of hoots and hollers came from a few of his friends.

Maya scowled before turning back to the Grayfall Guardian. "Do you live around here?"

"All my life. I protect these here woods. Someone's gotta."

"Protect them from what?" another man asked.

"Predators." The word hung in the air.

"Predators?" someone echoed. "What exactly have we gotten ourselves into? Did you guys hire this lunatic to add to the backwoods experience? Please tell me you did."

"No, sir," Max said, lifting his radio to call this in. "We did not. But we have every right to use this trail. And the county gave us permission to use Grayfall. We're paying a pretty penny for it. Not only that, but we hired locals to help us set up. We gave them jobs where there weren't any. You guys should be grateful."

"Grateful, my foot." Grayfall Guardian turned to the crowd, his weathered face grave with unspoken knowledge. "I reckon at least some of y'all got good sense, so listen up. Y'all are fixin' to head into somethin' you don't wanna mess with in them thar hills. Still time to hightail it back to wherever y'all came from afore it's too late."

With that cryptic warning, he and his friends melted back into the forest as suddenly as they'd appeared. They left the group staring at the empty trail and wondering what exactly they were walking into.

But all Olive could think about was the possibility that this man—someone who kept an eye on everything going on in this area—might know something about Chloe.

CHAPTER 19

The silence that followed Grayfall Guardian's departure stretched uncomfortably long, broken only by the sound of shifting backpacks and the nervous clearing of throats.

Olive watched Max's face cycle through expressions—annoyance, calculation, and finally a forced return to his professional guide persona. He lowered his radio after calling in the incident.

"Well, that was interesting." His laugh sounded hollow in the mountain air. "You get all kinds of characters living back in these hollers—old-timers who've been here so long they start seeing ghosts in every shadow."

"He seemed pretty specific about Grayfall." Dr. Z studied the forest where the man had vanished. "What did he mean about things that don't belong?

I've covered festivals in remote locations before, and locals usually support the surge in the economy."

"Mountain folklore." Sorrel moved closer to the group's center. "These old mining towns have been abandoned for decades. People start telling stories to keep outsiders away. They want to protect their territory. That's all."

Olive noticed how both guides kept glancing toward the forest where the man had vanished, their casual dismissals not matching their obvious tension. This wasn't their first encounter with people like the Grayfall Guardian, was it?

As Max shifted, Olive caught sight of the gun in his waistband.

Her chest constricted.

Had he brought it to keep this group safe? Or to keep them in line?

She didn't want to find out.

The woman who'd hurt her ankle waved her hand in the air to get people's attention. "Maybe we should listen to him? I mean, he lives here. Maybe he knows something we don't."

"He probably knows that scaring tourists is a good way to keep his favorite fishing spots secret," Max interrupted. "Trust me, locals around here have been pulling this kind of nonsense for generations."

Olive caught Jason's eye and saw her own skepticism reflected in his gaze.

The guides were working too hard to dismiss the warning. Their explanations felt rehearsed rather than genuine.

Sorrel consulted his watch. "We're already behind schedule. The opening ceremony starts in three hours, and we still have another hour of hiking ahead of us."

"Opening ceremony?" Maya held up her phone despite the poor signal. "I thought the first performances didn't start until eight. My content calendar is totally based on that schedule."

"You know, the welcome activities," Max explained. "They'll start around six, along with a cookout. There will be a Meet and Greet with some of the artists, vendor booths, that sort of thing. You'll want to get settled in your accommodations before things begin."

"Won't the other groups who left behind us be late?" someone else asked.

"We'll fill them in."

Tevin quietly observed the exchange while adjusting his hiking boots. Then he stood and shouldered his pack. "Well, I'm ready to see what all the fuss is about. We've come too far to turn back now. This is exactly the kind of authentic experience I cover on my podcast. In fact, I think some ghosts might make this even more memorable."

His words seemed to break the spell of uncertainty that had settled over the group. Other hikers began adjusting their packs and preparing to continue, though Olive noticed several people still glancing nervously toward the forest as if expecting the Grayfall Guardian and his friends to appear again and ambush everyone.

"That's the spirit." Max's shoulders dropped as the tension drained from his face. "Follow me, everyone. The best part of the journey is still ahead."

Olive wasn't so sure that was true.

As the group began hiking again, Olive felt sweat trickling from her temples and down her back. It was hot out here, and her water was almost gone. Max had said there was a stream where they could refill, but she'd seen the water there.

It looked muddy. No way was she drinking that. She didn't see anyone else drinking it either. If they did, Olive hoped they were prepared to have stomach issues later today.

The weight of her backpack was beginning to make her back ache.

She was in shape, so she could only imagine how some of the people who weren't as active were doing.

Three other groups should have left the lodge

already, no doubt with their own "guides" with them.

Were their guides more friendly than Max, Sorrel, and Tom?

For their sakes, she hoped so.

As Jason began chatting with Max—probably a strategic move—she fell into step beside the woman who'd hurt her ankle. She'd fallen back toward the end of the group and was among the last stragglers.

"Is your ankle okay?" Olive whispered.

"I guess." The girl's voice carried doubt. "It's just . . . my grandmother always said to listen when locals give you warnings. They know things outsiders don't. She went to the ocean once, and a local warned her about the riptides there. She didn't listen and almost drowned. Another woman warned my whole family not to eat at a restaurant in town. We did anyway and got food poisoning. Now, I always listen."

Something about her words caused a chill to wash over Olive.

"I'm Olivia, by the way. What's your name?"

"Becca. Becca Morrison. I'm a journalism student at West Virginia University." She paused before adding, "I'm actually here working on a research paper about music festivals and their impact on rural communities."

"Find anything interesting in your research?" Olive tried to sound casual as she asked the question.

"Not yet. I'm just starting."

"Why start with Grayfall?" Olive asked.

"It sounded interesting."

Olive couldn't help but think there was more to her story. "You ever heard of the guy who's organizing this festival before? Brad Something?"

"Kellerman," she answered, something hardening in her voice. "As a matter of fact, I have. He's started numerous companies before."

"Do most of his companies have something to do with music?"

"No, he's been all over the place—everything from new apps to technology. One thing is for sure. He leaves a trail of destruction wherever he goes."

Olive raised her eyebrows. "Is that right? Like what?"

Becca glanced around to make sure the guides weren't listening, then leaned closer. "Like there was this one girl who worked for him back in Tennessee. She hasn't been seen since her internship ended."

Olive's pulse spiked. "I had no idea."

She truly hadn't heard about this yet. It seemed like something that would have popped up in her research.

Becca's voice dropped lower. "People said she just

left early, but her family swears she never made it home."

Olive's pulse continued to pound harder, faster. "What do you think happened to her?"

"I wish I knew."

Olive didn't like the sound of that.

Why hadn't she seen anything about this other missing woman in her research? She'd been thorough.

It was definitely something she needed to look into . . . if she ever got a signal on her phone.

Just then, a scream cut through the air.

Something else had happened . . . but what now?

CHAPTER 20

Maya—of course it was Maya again—paused on the path and pointed to something off the trail. "Look at that!"

Olive pushed herself to the front of the line so she could see.

Her breath caught.

There was a rocky outcropping there. And in the center of one of the biggest boulders was blood. What appeared to be *fresh* blood.

All her instincts went on alert.

Max pushed his way to the front of the crowd also, and his eyes narrowed when he saw the red on the rock.

"It's nothing to be alarmed about," he announced. "Probably just a hunter processing his prize."

"There are hunters out here?" someone else asked.

"Yes, of course there are hunters," Max responded. "We're a big enough group that they should be aware of us. But I'm sure that's just what that blood is about."

Olive would bet it wasn't.

From across the crowd, she and Jason exchanged a look.

"Now, come on," Max said. "Let's keep going."

He tried to continue herding people toward the festival site. But Olive remained near the blood another moment, her gaze sweeping over everything.

That was when her eyes stopped on what looked like a bracelet that had fallen off in between the rocks.

Using her phone, she pretended like she was taking a picture of the blood. But really, it was the bracelet. She needed to make sure that Chloe hadn't worn one like that.

Jason joined her again. They had so much to talk about.

They just needed some privacy first.

As the path descended more steeply, Olive thought she saw a clearing in the distance. Grayfall? Part of her couldn't wait to get there so she could dig more deeply into Chloe's disappearance. Not to mention her legs were getting tired and she was hungry after eating that sad excuse for a sandwich. She could imagine everyone else felt the same.

"Hey." Jason pointed above them as a chopping sound filled the air. "Look at that."

Olive followed his gaze. A helicopter flew overhead.

"I wonder if one of the bands is inside?" Olive questioned.

"Possibly. Looks like a nice copter. Expensive."

"I imagine the budget for this event had to be pretty big." She paused. "Not that you would guess that based on the lunch they packed for us."

"I know, right? I could eat better in prison."

They came to one of the downed trees blocking the road. It was large, but it wouldn't have been that difficult for someone to make a path through.

How interesting that festival organizers hadn't done that. It would have made things so much easier if they could ride in something.

As Jason helped Olive over, she lowered her voice and asked, "Did Max say anything interesting?"

"He did, as a matter of fact." Jason released her hand as she stood on flat ground again. "He said he's been working for festival organizers for two months now, and he hasn't been paid for his work here yet."

She narrowed her eyes. "Really? I'm surprised he's still doing his job then."

"I heard they're being promised their backpay plus a big bonus when this is done."

"Sounds like a trainwreck."

"Tell me about it."

The pieces of the puzzle were starting to form a picture, and Olive didn't like what she was seeing.

The warning from the Grayfall Guardian suddenly felt less like superstition and more like a lifeline they'd just chosen to ignore.

Because something was wrong with this whole setup.

The trail opened into a clearing that looked nothing like the promotional videos Olive had studied before arriving.

Where the glossy brochure had promised a "transformed historic mining town hosting an immersive musical experience," the reality was a ghost town that time and weather had been slowly devouring for decades.

Grayfall spread before them like a movie set for a post-apocalyptic film. The main street—if the cracked strip of asphalt could still be called that—was flanked by the hollow shells of what had once been a thriving community.

A two-story building sagged under the weight of a partially collapsed roof, its broken windows staring out like dead eyes. Faded paint on the brick facade still spelled out "Grayfall Mercantile" in letters that were more ghost than substance.

Next to it, the skeletal remains of what appeared to be a drugstore stood with its front door hanging askew on rusted hinges. The pharmacy sign had fallen and shattered across the front steps, scattered among decades of accumulated leaves and debris. Across the street, a diner's neon sign dangled from a single wire, its cheerful promise of "Home-Cooked Meals" rendered grotesque by the vines that had grown through its broken letters.

Other buildings lined the street in various stages of decay—a post office with its roof caved in, a small church whose steeple listed dangerously to one side, houses whose front porches had collapsed into piles of rotting timber.

Rusted cars from the seventies and eighties sat where they'd been abandoned, their windows smashed, and their bodies slowly being reclaimed by kudzu and Virginia creeper.

But it was the backdrop that made the scene truly ominous.

Rising behind the town like the mouth of some

ancient beast was the entrance to the old coal mine. It yawned black and forbidding in the mountainside.

Twisted metal support beams framed the opening, and a faded warning sign that was too distant to read hung at an angle. Railway tracks, rusted orange with age, emerged from the mine entrance and disappeared into the undergrowth.

The promotional videos had somehow made this look magical and atmospheric.

In person, it felt like stepping into a place where hope had come to die.

CHAPTER 21

"Welcome to Grayfall Festival!" Max turned and announced with what sounded like forced enthusiasm. "Your home for the next three days!"

The group stood in stunned silence, taking in the scene before them.

"Is that . . . is that the main stage?" Maya held her phone high as she tried to capture the scene for her followers. Her voice made it clear she was disappointed.

What had been advertised as a "main stage with a state-of-the-art sound system" was actually a wooden platform that looked like it had been assembled that morning. There were visible gaps between the boards, and the speakers appeared to have been borrowed from a high school gymnasium.

"It's what we call an intimate acoustic setting," Max said. "This was created to give you the ultimate backwoods experience. It matches the areas where many of these artists grew up. Besides, it's got a much better sound quality than those massive corporate festivals. You'll feel like you're in the artists' living room."

Artists' living room? That was a good one. Some people might even buy it.

"And over there," Tom gestured toward a cluster of tents, "are your glamping accommodations."

Olive stared at the area. It was located beside the river that ran through town, in what probably used to be a park. However, if someone started sleepwalking at night, they were likely to walk right off the steep banks and into the rapids.

It seemed like a terrible idea.

"Each site comes with premium camping gear and all the amenities you'll need for a comfortable wilderness experience," Tom finished, sounding as if he'd memorized a script.

Her gaze went from the area where the tents were set up to the tents themselves.

The "glamping" accommodations were clearly just regular camping tents with equipment that looked like it had been rented in bulk from a discount outdoor store. No platforms, no electricity, no luxury amenities—just circles of trampled earth with Coleman tents and basic camp chairs.

"Wait." The obnoxious frat boy who'd mentioned moonshine earlier stepped from the crowd. "I paid for luxury. This is just . . . rustic camping."

"Luxury is relative." Max's smile looked more strained than it had a few minutes earlier. "You're surrounded by pristine wilderness, breathing clean mountain air, sleeping under the stars. That's worth more than any fancy hotel room."

Maya frantically hit buttons on her phone. "I'm still not getting any signal. My phone shows full bars, but nothing's loading. How am I supposed to stream parts of this to my followers?"

"Mountain terrain can be tricky for cell service," Sorrel explained. "That's part of the digital detox experience we advertised. It's time to disconnect from the outside world and reconnect with music and nature."

As he said the words, the helicopter rose in the distance, cutting into the supposedly gentle sounds of nature. It appeared the band had been delivered.

Someone beside her muttered something about wishing they could catch a ride.

As the copter lifted away and out of sight, Olive pulled out her own phone and confirmed Maya's observation. The signal strength indicator showed excellent coverage, but nothing would load. No texts, no calls, no internet. It was as if the phones were receiving a signal that led nowhere.

She let out a frustrated grunt. This was even worse than she thought.

"And over there is where our cookout will take place." Max pointed to a large white tent set up in what was probably a public parking lot at one time. "Help yourself to the food that's been prepared."

Before anyone could ask any more questions, a commotion near the food tent drew their attention. A small crowd had broken off from the "orientation" session and gathered inside—probably hungry after their long hike and meager lunch.

Their voices rose in complaint.

"What do you mean you're only serving hot dogs?" someone shouted. "Hot dogs? There's nothing gourmet about hot dogs. I'm hungry, and it's dinnertime! Where's my steak?"

The next moment, chaos broke loose.

Olive moved closer, Jason by her side.

She needed to know what was going on.

Inside the tent, plastic picnic tables had been set up in rows. At the back, there were banquet tables where food was being served. A man in a white chef's hat seemed to be taking the brunt of people's complaints.

"Sorry, folks," the man said. "Our supplies are running late. This is all we've got right now."

Maya pushed through the crowd, her composure finally cracking. "This is ridiculous! My followers are going to absolutely roast this place!"

"There's plenty of food." An edge of defensiveness filled the chef's tone. "Hot dogs may not be ideal, but it's what we've got until we get our next delivery."

"What did you do?" Frat Boy yelled. "Forget to pay your vendors or something?"

Olive watched the scene unfold with growing unease. The food situation wasn't just disappointing —it was potentially dangerous. If people were stranded here for three days with inadequate provisions and no way to leave . . .

"Ladies and gentlemen!" A new voice cut through the complaints.

Olive turned to see a man in his forties climb on top of one of the tables.

Before he said his name, she knew exactly who he was.

He was the man at the top of her suspect list.

CHAPTER 22

"I'm Brad Kellerman, festival director, and I want to personally welcome you to what's going to be the most unique musical experience of your lives!"

The crowd turned toward the man, their complaints temporarily set aside.

Olive studied Brad. He carried himself with the confident swagger of someone accustomed to getting his way. He was tall and lean with graying hair that made him look distinguished rather than old, and he had the kind of sharp features that could be handsome or menacing depending on his mood. His clothes were expensive but practical—designer outdoor wear that actually looked lived-in.

She would guess him to be in his early fifties . . . would put him close to the same age as her father if he were still alive.

Had the two ever met? She stowed the question away in the back of her mind.

"Now, I know some of you might be feeling a little . . . *surprised* by our setup here." Brad's smile never wavered. "But that's exactly the point! We're not trying to recreate some corporate mega-festival. We're creating something authentic, something real, something that connects you directly to the music and the natural world around you."

"Where are the headliners?" someone called from the crowd. "The schedule said Midnight Echo is supposed to perform tonight. Are they here? Do they have better accommodations than us?"

"Ah, yes." Brad's smile dimmed. "We'll have some updates for you soon. In the meantime, grab a bite to eat and get settled in your tents. Then we'll meet back here in an hour for our unforgettable festival to begin!"

The murmurs from the crowd were decidedly less enthusiastic.

Olive thought about the Grayfall Guardian's cryptic warning. Looking around at the hastily assembled stage, the basic camping setup, and the strangely jammed cell service, she was beginning to understand what he'd meant about things that didn't belong.

This wasn't a music festival. It was a trap.

And they were all caught in it.

But the question was—why?

"Site twelve." Max consulted his clipboard as he led Olive and Jason down a path between the camping areas. "Your luxury wilderness suite."

He gestured toward what could generously be called a campsite—a patch of trampled earth near the river, surrounded by other sites that felt entirely too close. In the center sat a two-person dome tent that looked like it had been purchased from a thrift store's clearance rack. The olive-green nylon was already showing signs of wear, with a visible patch of duct tape covering what was probably a hole near the bottom.

Bathrooms? They consisted of a row of portable toilets set up on the edge of the campground. Apparently, showers weren't an option.

Gross.

"This is it?" Jason's voice carried the perfect note of disappointed confusion that their cover story required.

"Premium camping experience." Max's enthusiasm sounded forced. "You've got your shelter, camp chairs, and a designated fire ring." He pointed to a circle of rocks that looked like they'd been pulled from the river and hastily arranged that morning. "Everything you need for an authentic wilderness adventure."

Olive stepped closer to examine their accommodations. The tent was smaller than it had appeared in the promotional photos—barely large enough for two sleeping bags, let alone the comfortable bedding that had been promised. Two flimsy camp chairs sat beside a plastic storage bin that presumably contained their "luxury amenities."

She lifted the lid of the bin and found a single battery-powered lantern, two thin sleeping bags that crinkled like they were stuffed with newspaper, and a package of generic granola bars.

"This is disappointing." Though she was undercover, her words were sincere.

This was honestly shocking—even worse than she'd imagined. If she'd actually paid for this, she would be furious.

Max's smile became more strained. "Like I said, luxury is relative out here. You're sleeping under the stars, breathing pure mountain air—"

"For five thousand dollars," Jason interrupted, his eyebrows suspended. "We paid five thousand dollars each to be here this weekend."

Max's expression hardened slightly. "You're paying for the experience, not just the accommodations. Wait until you hear the music tonight. It will blow your mind."

Olive had serious doubts.

This whole festival was a disaster—in more than one way.

CHAPTER 23

After Max left, Olive and Jason stood in awkward silence, staring at their pathetic campsite.

Around them, other festivalgoers were discovering similar disappointments, their voices carrying through the air in various stages of disbelief and anger.

"Well . . ." Jason finally said as he stared at their tent. "This is cozy."

Cozy was an understatement. The tent was tiny with barely enough room for both of them. Sleeping at night would be more awkward than she'd imagined.

Not only that, but she was kind of hungry. She'd grabbed a hot dog earlier, but it wouldn't hold her over for long.

Olive dropped her voice to barely above a whisper. "We need to talk, but not here." She glanced around at the neighboring campsites, noting how sound would carry in the open area. "Too many ears."

Jason nodded. "Later."

They spent the next few minutes setting up their pitiful accommodations.

Finally, when she was confident they weren't being watched too closely, she unzipped the tent and crawled inside. Jason followed, and for a moment they were alone in the dim interior of what was supposed to be their luxury suite.

"This is a disaster." Olive kept her voice so low it was almost inaudible. "But that's not the worst part."

Jason settled beside her in the cramped space, close enough that she could feel his warmth. She ignored the fact that her heart began to pound faster.

"What did you find in Elias's office?" Jason asked.

"Incident reports going back years. Missing person cases, search and rescue operations that turned up nothing." She pulled out her phone and found the photos she'd taken earlier. "There have been way more disappearances than just the three we knew about. And all the reports have notes in the margins—things like 'too close to Grayfall' and 'ignored safety protocols.'"

He pressed his lips into a tight line before saying,

"So someone has been covering up these incidents for a long time."

"That's what it looks like. Plus, remember the man on the trail?" Olive shivered despite the warm air inside the tent. "I think he knows something we don't."

Jason's expression tightened. "What kind of something are you thinking he knows?"

"I don't know yet. But between his warning, the missing person reports, and this joke of a festival—" She gestured around their pathetic accommodations. "I think we're dealing with something a lot more dangerous than financial fraud."

"You think they're planning to—"

Before Jason could finish his thought, voices erupted outside their tent. Loud, angry voices that suggested other festivalgoers had reached their breaking point with the accommodations.

Olive and Jason exchanged glances. This could be the distraction they needed to do more investigating, or it could be the moment everything fell apart completely.

"We should see what's happening." Olive already reached for the tent's zipper.

Whatever was about to unfold, she had a feeling it would reveal more about what they were really dealing with in Grayfall.

When Olive and Jason emerged from their tent, she saw that a crowd had gathered in the center of the festival grounds.

The volume of complaints grew by the minute, and even from a distance, Olive could see that people were beyond frustrated.

They were furious.

"This is absolutely unacceptable!" Maya's voice cut through the general murmur of discontent. She stood near the front of the crowd, her phone held high as she documented the scene for her followers. "I paid five thousand dollars for luxury glamping, and they gave me a tent that smells like mildew and a sleeping bag that's probably older than I am!"

A chorus of agreement rose from the crowd. People held up their phones to document the area and show off the deplorable accommodations. They compared notes about missing amenities and false advertising.

"Where's the gourmet food we were promised?" called out an older man in a cowboy hat. "Catering ran out of everything except granola bars!"

"And what about the spa services?" added a woman who looked like she'd never been camping in her life. "The website specifically mentioned massage therapy and wellness treatments!"

Connor held his camera, recording the crowd's anger and the stark reality of their surroundings.

Dr. Z stood at the edge of the crowd, a scowl on his face. He was probably mentally calculating the financial loss he was going to take on this.

That was when Brad Kellerman appeared again. He climbed onto the stage with his arms raised in a gesture that was probably meant to be calming but came across as condescending.

"Folks, folks!" His voice carried across the crowd. "I understand some of you have concerns about the accommodations—"

"Concerns?" Maya stepped forward, still filming. "These aren't concerns, these are straight-up lies! You advertised luxury wilderness experiences and delivered summer camp rejects!"

The crowd roared its agreement, and Brad's smile became more strained. "I know it's not what you expected. But remember, you're paying for authenticity. Real wilderness experience. Connection with nature that you can't get at some corporate resort—"

"For five thousand dollars?" another man called out. "I could have gone to an actual luxury resort for less than this!"

"When does the music start?" someone from the back of the crowd called out. "At least tell me Midnight Echo is still performing tonight! Aren't we supposed to have a meet and greet?"

Brad paused for a second too long—long enough for Olive to know what was coming.

"Well . . ." His smile faltered. "I do have a small update about tonight's lineup."

The crowd's energy shifted from angry to dangerous.

"Midnight Echo has encountered some transportation issues getting their equipment to our remote location." Brad's voice pitched higher. "But we've arranged instead for some incredible local talent that really captures the authentic spirit of Appalachian music—"

"You've got to be kidding me!" Maya's voice cracked with disbelief. "Midnight Echo was the entire reason I came here!"

"Local talent?" An older man's face turned red. "I didn't pay thousands of dollars to hear some guy play hillbilly music with a banjo!"

The crowd grew more unhinged by the second. People shouted over each other, waved their phones, and demanded refunds that clearly weren't going to happen.

Olive noticed how Max, Sorrel, and Tom had positioned themselves around the perimeter of the crowd. If she had to guess, they'd done so not to help manage the situation, but to prevent anyone from leaving. Six other men had joined them as new groups had arrived.

"Now, now." Brad held up his hands. "I know change can be difficult, but I promise you that tonight's performances are going to be unlike anything you've experienced—"

"Because they're going to suck!" someone yelled.

"This is already unlike anything I've ever experienced!" another voice yelled. "And not in a good way. We want our money back."

"I want to speak to whoever's really in charge here!"

Olive caught Jason's eye and saw her own thoughts reflected there.

If the crowd kept escalating like this, she had a feeling they were about to find out exactly what Brad meant when he said tonight would be "unlike anything they'd experienced."

The question was whether any of them would survive to tell about it.

CHAPTER 24

An hour later, event staff was still working to appease angry concert goers.

Not only was all the food gone, but people had also discovered the toilets were already stinky. Restlessness amongst concertgoers continued to grow.

Finally, as the sun began to set behind the mountains, casting long shadows across the crumbling town of Grayfall, the stage lights flickered on.

The crowd gathered in front of the wooden platform, their earlier frustration simmering into resigned disappointment.

"Ladies and gentlemen." Brad's voice crackled through the pathetic sound system. "Please welcome . . . the Mountain Boys!"

Three men in their fifties shuffled onto the stage carrying well-used instruments. The banjo player's shirt was stained, the fiddle player kept adjusting his baseball cap nervously, and the guitarist couldn't seem to find a comfortable way to hold his beat-up acoustic.

They launched into what might generously be called bluegrass. In reality, it sounded more like three people who'd learned different songs and decided to play them simultaneously. The banjo was out of tune, the fiddle screeched on the high notes, and the guitarist's timing was so off it was painful.

Olive forced herself to smile and nod along, playing the part of a supportive festivalgoer while internally cringing at every off-key note. Around her, other attendees were checking their phones, shifting uncomfortably, or staring at the decrepit buildings surrounding them with expressions that suggested they were questioning every life choice that had brought them here.

She used the performance as cover to study the crowd. First, her gaze found Tevin. He was on the other side of the group, near Becca. The two of them laughed together about something.

Perfect. He was usually a behind the scenes guy, but there was no way he'd be able to do his normal duties in this place. Still, she wanted to keep an eye on him. He was like a brother to her and one of her closest friends. She wouldn't be able to live with herself if something happened to him.

Three more groups had arrived throughout the afternoon, bringing their numbers close to four hundred. At least one more group should still be hiking in.

She prayed that group didn't encounter any problems.

What if the Grayfall Guardian and his crew had threatened them also—and then carried through with it?

With generators humming in the background, her gaze swept across the faces illuminated by the stage lights. Something cold settled in her stomach.

High in the mountains, she was nearly certain there were people watching this festival unfold. Not concertgoers.

Dark Watchers? Or was Maya getting into her head too much?

She didn't know, but she didn't like the feeling in her gut.

As the banjo player hit a particularly sour note, several people in the crowd visibly winced.

That was when she saw movement in the woods.

She wasn't imagining things.

Someone was out there.

"Something's wrong." Olive leaned toward Jason so her words wouldn't carry.

"The music? Yeah, it's terrible."

"Not the music. Someone is watching us from the woods."

Jason's eyes swept the area, and she saw the moment he spotted what she'd noticed. His jaw tightened.

"You're right," he murmured. "I see at least two people."

The Mountain Boys launched into their version of "Foggy Mountain Breakdown," though it sounded more like "Broken Mountain Disaster." Olive tried to focus on the performance, but her skin crawled.

Connor stood near the front of the crowd, his camera capturing the trainwreck performance from multiple angles. As the festival's videographer, he might have additional footage from the promotional shoots, she realized.

Since Chloe had been involved in the promotional video, Connor might have hours of behind-the-scenes content that could provide clues about what was going on here.

But approaching him would have to wait. Too many eyes were on the crowd right now.

The song—if it could be called that—finally wheezed to a conclusion, and scattered applause rippled through the audience. Most people looked like they were clapping out of politeness rather than appreciation.

"Thank y'all, thank y'all!" the banjo player called, his grin revealing several missing teeth. "Y'all are a wonderful audience! We got a few more songs for ya before we take a little break."

A collective groan rose from several festivalgoers.

Olive settled in for what was clearly going to be a long, painful evening. But her mind was racing. Whatever Chloe had discovered in this creepy ghost town, it had been enough to make her send that final, cryptic text.

There's more to Grayfall than you think. The trees are watching.

Now Olive was beginning to understand what Chloe meant.

It wasn't just the trees that were watching—it was everyone.

And time was running out to figure out why before she and Jason became the next people to disappear in these mountains.

CHAPTER 25

The Mountain Boys were on intermission when more chaos erupted at the back of the crowd.

"Someone was in my tent!" Maya's voice cut through the murmurs of the crowd as she ran toward the stage area, her face pale with shock and anger. "Someone went through my stuff in my tent!"

Heads turned toward the commotion. Maya, who clearly wasn't shy, climbed onto the stage and stood in the glow of the stage lights. Her perfectly styled hair was now disheveled, and her hands shook as she held up her phone.

"I went back to get my portable charger." Her voice carried clearly in the sudden silence. "My tent was torn apart. My backpack was open. My clothes were everywhere. Someone went through everything."

Murmurs of concern and fear rippled through the crowd.

"I think it was the Mothman," she finished.

The Mothman? Really?

"Why would you think that?" Dr. Z asked.

"When I went inside, I thought I saw glowing red eyes. The Mothman has those, right?"

Brad Kellerman appeared at Maya's side with the speed of someone who'd been expecting this.

"Now, now, let's not panic." His voice lilted in attempted reassurance. "Sometimes animals can get into tents if food is left out—"

"This wasn't an animal!" Maya's composure had completely disappeared. "My stuff was searched, not destroyed. Someone was looking for something specific."

"What kind of something?" a man yelled.

"I don't know! But they looked through my memory cards, my laptop bag, my—" She stopped abruptly, her face going even paler. "Oh no. My backup hard drive. I didn't see it. I think it's been stolen."

The crowd's energy shifted from concern to genuine fear.

If someone was bold enough to search tents while everyone was gathered for the performance, what else were they capable of?

"I'm sure it just got misplaced in the confusion."

Brad's smile was looking more strained by the minute. "These mountain campsites can be tricky—"

"I didn't misplace anything!" Maya's voice rose to near hysteria. "Someone deliberately went through my belongings and stole my equipment!"

Jason tensed beside Olive. If someone was searching tents, looking for cameras and recording devices, it suggested they were worried about documentation. About evidence.

"Has anyone else noticed anything missing?" Dr. Z asked. "You shouldn't leave valuables in these tents. They're not secure!"

The crowd started to fracture as people hurried back toward their campsites to assess their own situations.

"Please, everyone, let's stay calm." Brad's voice was quickly losing its authority. "I'm sure this is just a misunderstanding—"

"Like the misunderstanding about Midnight Echo?" Frat Boy yelled from the crowd. "Or the misunderstanding about the luxury accommodations? How about the food?"

The situation was deteriorating rapidly. People were scared, angry, and beginning to realize they might be trapped in a situation that was far more dangerous than they'd bargained for.

"Everything is under control," Brad called. "To make you feel better, drinks are on the house!"

People emerged from the catering tent carrying coolers and cups.

A collective cheer sounded.

As people scattered to get their drinks, Olive saw her opportunity. She gave a nod to Jason, indicating she should have this conversation alone. He headed back to their tent.

As he did, Olive approached Connor as he adjusted his camera settings, apparently preparing to document the aftermath of Maya's revelation.

"Excuse me. We haven't officially met, but I'm Olivia Jones. I wanted to tell you how impressed I am with the promotional video you created."

Connor looked up, his expression cautious but professional. "Thanks. Though this isn't exactly the festival footage I expected to be shooting."

"I bet it's not."

"However, they told me they wanted me to film everything." He shrugged. "I thought it was a little weird. But I'm just doing what they're paying me for."

Olive glanced around to make sure they weren't being observed too closely. "I'm actually curious about the promotional videos I saw. The production quality was incredible. You must have hours of footage from those shoots."

Connor's laugh sounded bitter. "Hours and hours. And what a complete disaster that was."

"Disaster?" Her curiosity was real and pressing.

"The whole promotional shoot was insane. They hired people to come party for the cameras, flew in cases of alcohol, and basically threw a massive rager. I filmed it to make this place look like the hottest festival destination in the country." Connor shook his head. "Most of the 'festivalgoers' in those videos were paid actors, completely wasted by noon."

Olive's pulse quickened. "Everyone was drunk?"

"Most people, yeah. It was like a frat party, not a professional video shoot." Connor paused, studying her face. "Why do you ask?"

"I'm curious about someone from the video. That blonde girl who talked about the festival being a 'transformation'? I was hoping to get her name, to see if she might be interested in being in an advertisement for my business. I have a line of all-natural skin care products. I'd love to talk to you about utilizing your services as well."

"You mean Chloe?" Connor's expression shifted, becoming more guarded.

"Is that her name? I haven't seen her here at the actual festival. I was hoping I might."

Connor remained quiet for a long moment, and when he spoke, his voice was lower. "Chloe got mad and left. Can't say I blame her."

"She left? Why?" Olive tried to keep her tone casual, just curious rather than investigative. "What happened?"

Connor glanced around as if checking to see who might be listening. "The last time I saw her, she was going to explore the old mine."

Olive held her breath, anxious to hear what else he had to say. "Why would she do that?"

Maybe she and Jason would get their first real lead.

Then he stopped abruptly, his face closing off. "I probably shouldn't—"

"Connor!" Brad's voice cut through their conversation like a blade. "I need you to get some crowd control footage. Document how well we're handling this situation."

Connor's expression became carefully neutral. "Sure thing, Brad. Be right there."

He turned back to Olive, but the openness was gone from his face. "Nice talking to you, Mrs. Jones. Enjoy the rest of the festival."

As he walked toward Brad, frustration built in Olive's chest.

Connor knew something—something about what had made Chloe angry enough to leave the promotional shoot. Something that might explain what she'd discovered about Grayfall.

And now Olive needed to figure out where Connor was storing all that extra footage.

Because if Chloe had seen something that revealed the truth about this place, it might be the key to understanding what had really happened to her.

The question was how to get access to hours of video footage without blowing her cover or ending up like the people in Elias's incident reports—another missing person case with no satisfactory resolution.

CHAPTER 26

As Olive and Jason found each other near the stage, ready to discuss what Connor had revealed, a bright voice interrupted them. "Oh my goodness, you two are so cute!"

Maya appeared beside them, swaying slightly as she held her phone with one hand and a plastic cup with the other. Her once perfectly applied makeup was now smudged around her eyes, and her words carried the telltale slur of someone who'd been drinking to forget their problems.

"I'm sorry, what?" Olive asked, momentarily thrown off by the interruption and by the change in Maya's demeanor.

"You guys! The way you're looking at each other—it's like, relationship goals, you know?" Maya giggled, the sound slightly too loud and too long. "I have to get this for my story. My followers are going to die for some authentic couple content."

How much alcohol had Maya consumed? They'd only started serving it fifteen minutes ago. Could she already be inebriated?

Olive saw festival staff still moving between groups of disgruntled attendees, still offering plastic cups filled with what appeared to be beer and mixed drinks.

Free alcohol, apparently, to help people forget about the missing headliners, terrible accommodations, and general disaster the festival had become.

"I see they're giving out free drinks." Jason kept his voice neutral.

"Yeah!" Maya waved her cup enthusiastically, sloshing liquid over the rim. "Brad said it was their way of apologizing for the 'logistical challenges.' Super generous, right? I got the good stuff—moonshine!"

Olive and Jason exchanged a look. Getting a crowd of angry, disappointed people drunk seemed like the opposite of a good idea. Unless, of course, you wanted people to be less capable of clear thinking and coordinated action.

And this moonshine must be really strong.

"That's . . . thoughtful of them." Olive swallowed hard, everything inside her rebelling against what was happening here.

"Right? Anyway, can I please film you guys being adorable? I need some positive content after everything that's happened today." Maya held up her phone, already switching it to video mode. "Just act natural and cute together. My audience loves authentic relationship moments."

Olive's pulse spiked. Being filmed was the last thing she wanted right now, but refusing might look suspicious. And Maya was clearly intoxicated enough that arguing with her might create more of a scene.

"I guess that would be okay." Olive forced a smile.

"Perfect!" She held her phone higher. "Just pretend I'm not here and be yourselves."

Pretending *not* to be herself was what Olive did best.

Jason stepped closer, and Olive wrapped her arms around his waist.

The moment their bodies touched, warmth flooded through her system. Even through the stress of their investigation, even with all the unresolved tension between them, her body still responded to his nearness like they were teenagers again.

She wanted to melt into him, to forget about

missing persons and fake festivals and all the reasons she'd been keeping him at arm's length. The familiar scent of his woodsy cologne, the solid warmth of his chest against her cheek, the way his arms came up to circle her shoulders—it all felt like coming home.

But she couldn't let herself go there. Not now. Not when so much was at stake.

"You're so beautiful," Jason murmured.

The soft undertone of his words made Olive's pulse flutter.

"Stop." She giggled. "You're just saying that for the camera."

"I'm saying it because it's true." He pressed a gentle kiss to her forehead.

Olive had to fight not to close her eyes at the tenderness of the gesture. She longed for moments like these—but not fake ones.

Real ones.

"This is perfect!" Maya gushed from behind her phone. "You guys are like, couple goals for real. Tell my followers how excited you are to be at Grayfall!"

The woman seemed to have forgotten about how upset she'd been earlier. The alcohol was working wonders with her attitude.

Jason's arm tightened around Olive's shoulders.

"We're looking forward to seeing how this plays out." His voice sounded bright and convincing. "The setting is incredible, the music has been . . . unique, and getting to experience it all with my wife makes it even better."

"And we can't forget how beautiful the mountains are." Olive surprised herself by how steady her voice sounded. "And the festival has been full of surprises."

That was certainly true, though not in the way Maya's followers would expect.

"Aw, you're making me cry." Maya lowered her phone. "That's exactly the kind of content I needed. You guys are the best. I can't post any of this yet—I don't have a signal. But I'm going to have enough content for a month!"

She stumbled slightly as she turned away, and Olive wondered how much alcohol the festival organizers had distributed. If Maya was this intoxicated after such a short period of time, what would the crowd be like by the end of the evening?

"Thanks for letting me film," Maya called over her shoulder as she wandered toward another group of festivalgoers, presumably looking for more content.

Olive and Jason remained in their embrace for a moment longer, both of them reluctant to break the contact.

Finally, Jason's arms loosened, and Olive stepped back, immediately missing his warmth.

"That was interesting." She tried to sound casual.

"Getting everyone drunk is a classic crowd control technique." Jason's gaze darkened with disapproval. "Harder to organize, harder to think clearly, harder to make coordinated decisions about leaving."

"Exactly what I was thinking." Olive glanced at the festivalgoers who were already getting sloshed. "Whatever they're planning, they want to make us as compliant as possible."

"The question is what happens next?"

Olive thought about Connor's abrupt departure with Brad, about Maya's stolen hard drive, and about the watchers positioned around the crowd.

And this weekend had only just begun.

CHAPTER 27

By midnight, the festival grounds had quieted some.

The Mountain Boys had mercifully ended their torture session hours ago. Their bonfire hadn't been well attended—but that wasn't a surprise. Olive did wonder where the band was staying. She assumed it wasn't in these tents. Since they were locals, maybe they'd gone home for the night.

The watchers in the woods appeared to have disappeared . . . somewhere.

The free alcohol had done its job. Most of the attendees had either passed out in their tents or were too intoxicated to cause further trouble.

Olive and Jason had stayed outside observing and mingling.

But they hadn't seen anything that would help them find Chloe.

Not yet.

So they'd turned in for the night, vowing that tomorrow would be the day they found answers.

The inside of the tent was small—two uncomfortable air mattresses, each shoved into opposite walls of the tent. There was maybe a foot of space between them—just enough room to place their backpacks and shoes.

They had arranged their sleeping bags on top of the mattresses earlier and had set the single lantern near the entrance.

Olive lay on her bed, listening to Jason's steady breathing beside her. Sleep was impossible.

Every sound outside made her tense. The wind. The rushing water. The footsteps that probably belonged to guides—who'd since transformed into security guards.

"You awake?" Jason's whisper was so quiet she almost missed it.

"Yeah." She turned toward him in the darkness, acutely aware of how small their tent was, how close they were lying. "I can't stop thinking about what Connor said."

"About Chloe leaving the promotional shoot?"

"Yes. I need to know what he knows. I'm hoping I'll get the opportunity to talk to him tomorrow."

"He seems like a good source of information."

"And I keep thinking about the mine also." Olive shifted, and her arm brushed against Jason's. Even that slight contact sent electricity through her system. "It seems like the perfect place to hide something."

Jason was quiet a moment. "You want to check it out?"

The words she'd been waiting to hear . . .

"I think we have to," Olive whispered. "Connor indicated Chloe was headed there before she disappeared. It only makes sense."

"It could be where she is now."

The possibility hung between them like a prayer and a nightmare.

If Chloe was in the mine, she might still be alive. But she also might not be alone.

"It's risky," Jason said.

"Everything about this place is risky. But we can't just lie here and wait for something to happen to us too."

His gaze locked with hers. "Okay. But we do this together, and we're careful. If something feels wrong—"

"Then we get out immediately," she finished.

"Promise me."

The intensity in his voice made her turn toward him, though she could barely make out his features in the darkness. "I promise."

For a moment, they lay there in the dark. Olive felt hyperaware of everything—the warmth emanating from Jason, the way his presence made her feel both safer and more vulnerable at the same time, the way her soul longed for someone to share her life with.

"We should go now," she whispered, though part of her wanted to stay in this moment. "While everyone's drunk or asleep."

"Let's get moving." Jason sat up, ready to start.

But the weird ache remained in her chest.

Because she didn't really want to go to the mine.

She'd much rather stay here with Jason and pretend everything was fine between them. Like they could have a future together.

She'd been going solo at life for so long, and she hadn't realized just how weary she'd become.

Not until now.

Not until Jason.

Olive and Jason slipped out of their tent like shadows, moving with practiced stealth.

The festival grounds were mostly quiet. She heard the occasional snore from nearby tents. A few stragglers still laughed obnoxiously near the stage—the frat boy, if she had to guess. Empty plastic cups littered the common area, evidence of a hard night of partying.

She'd also noted the men patrolling the area.

For their safety? Or to keep people in line?

She still wasn't sure.

Olive and Jason had changed into black clothing and soft-soled shoes that would move silently over the rough terrain.

She couldn't help but notice how the moonlight caught the sharp angles of Jason's face, making him look both dangerous and incredibly attractive.

Focus, she told herself. *Missing girl. Potential crimes. This is* not *the time to be distracted by how good Jason looks.*

"You ready?" Jason asked.

She nodded. "Let's go."

They made their way through the camp, sticking to the shadows between abandoned buildings. The ruins of Grayfall looked even more ominous in the moonlight—skeletal remains of a once-thriving community, now serving as the backdrop for whatever sinister operation was unfolding here.

The mine entrance loomed ahead of them like a mouth ready to swallow whatever came too close. During the day, the place had looked merely abandoned. At night, it looked actively malevolent.

The entrance was larger than Olive had expected, easily wide enough for vehicles to pass through, and a fence with razor wire at the top stopped anyone from getting in.

"There." Jason pointed through the fence. "You see that?"

Olive squinted into the darkness and saw what he was indicating—a faint glow emanating from somewhere deep inside the tunnel, too steady and bright to be natural.

"Someone's down there," she whispered.

They stepped closer, every sense on high alert. The old warning signs were posted on the fence. "DANGER: UNSTABLE STRUCTURE" and "NO TRESPASSING" were painted in faded letters that should have deterred anyone with common sense.

If Olive was smart, she'd turn back now.

But she couldn't. She had a job to do.

CHAPTER 28

There was no way Olive was turning back—Jason either.

Instead they moved closer and closer to the mine.

As they did, Olive saw clear evidence that people had been ignoring those warnings to stay out—just as she suspected.

Fresh footprints marred the dirt around the entrance. Tire tracks from some kind of small vehicle. And most telling of all, a heavy-duty extension cord ran from a generator hidden behind a pile of old mining equipment into the depths of the tunnel.

"This is definitely not abandoned," Jason murmured.

Olive pulled out her phone and began photographing everything. The photos might be crucial evidence.

As they moved closer to the mine entrance, she spotted something that made her heart stop.

"Jason." Her voice was barely audible. "Look."

Caught on a piece of rusted metal near the entrance was a small piece of fabric—expensive-looking material in a distinctive shade of coral pink.

The same coral color Chloe was wearing in the promotional video.

Olive carefully freed it, her hands trembling. The fabric was high-quality silk, exactly the kind of thing a wealthy young woman like Chloe would wear.

"This could be proof that she was here, just like Connor mentioned." Olive's fingers closed around the material. "She may have gone inside the mine."

"The question is whether she made it back out."

Before Olive could respond, the sound of voices echoed from deep within the tunnel—male voices, speaking in low tones.

Olive and Jason froze, every instinct screaming at them to run. But the voices were their first real lead.

If Chloe was down there, if she was still alive, this might be their only chance to find her.

Jason's hand found Olive's in the darkness, squeezing gently. When she looked at him, his expression was resolute but worried.

They stepped closer to the entrance, closer toward whatever secrets Grayfall was hiding in its depths.

Olive and Jason were about to step into the mine entrance when the distant rumble of an engine made them both freeze.

Headlights from a small vehicle—an ATV—swept across the town, growing brighter as they approached the festival grounds.

"Someone's coming," Jason whispered.

The sound was getting closer—definitely headed their way.

If they were caught at the mine entrance, there would be no explaining what they were doing there in the middle of the night.

"We have to go." Olive pocketed the piece of fabric. "Now."

They melted back into the shadows just as an ATV rounded the corner, its headlights cutting through the darkness where they'd been standing moments before. Two figures were visible on the vehicle—one driving, one riding behind.

Olive couldn't make out their faces in the glare.

She and Jason crouched in the bushes.

As the ATV paused nearby, she heard a man say, "Make sure no one gets in here. We can't take that risk."

"Got it."

Olive was fairly certain it was one of the guides/guards. Maybe even Max.

The ATV moved farther down the trail.

"Security patrol," Jason breathed.

"We can't go back there tonight." Olive didn't bother to hide the frustration in her voice. "They'll be watching now. We got here a few minutes too late."

They waited until the ATV's engine faded before starting back to their tent. But as they moved through the shadows, something caught Olive's attention.

A warm glow emanated from beyond a cluster of pine trees behind the town.

"Look." She nodded toward the light.

Through the trees, they could see a large house. No, not just large. It was practically a mansion. Three stories with floor-to-ceiling windows that blazed with warm light.

It was around a bend in the mountain, which made it out of sight for anyone in town.

If she had to guess, this was one of the original houses in Grayfall—maybe where the owner of the mine had lived. Someone had restored it.

"We need to find out who's staying there," Jason said.

"I say we take a closer look."

Remaining low, they hurried toward the house. When they got close enough, they ducked behind some bushes, hoping to take in more details.

As they watched, a familiar figure appeared in one of the illuminated windows.

Brad Kellerman.

He gestured as he spoke to someone out of view, holding what appeared to be a glass of wine.

Olive's stomach tightened with disgust. While festival attendees were sleeping in threadbare tents with no running water, eating granola bars, wrestling with mosquitoes and flies, and dealing with nonexistent cell service, Brad was living like a king in what looked like a million-dollar vacation home.

"All that money people paid for tickets . . ." Anger tinged her voice. "And this is where it went."

"Not into the festival, that's for sure." Jason's voice hardened.

They watched another minute as more figures moved through the house—people who clearly weren't festival attendees, judging by their expensive clothing and casual demeanor.

Could Chloe be inside? Had the local police even searched the house? Had they talked to Brad?

That house was where the real party was happening, while everyone else suffered through the nightmare Brad had created.

"We need to get back." Reluctance filled Jason's voice. "Before anyone notices we're gone."

Olive took one last look at the mansion. Whatever

was happening at this festival, Brad was profiting handsomely from it.

But her gut told her there was more to this story than just one man wanting to get rich.

What she wasn't sure about was what.

As Olive walked back to their tent, she checked her phone one more time, hoping against hope for even a single bar of service.

Her phone showed full bars, but every attempt to send a message or make a call failed immediately.

"Still nothing," she whispered to Jason, slowing her steps. "I need to talk to Tevin, but there's no way to contact him. I'm not sure what tent he's in."

"Maybe we can find him somehow." Jason paused by their tent. As he examined the entrance flap, he frowned. "Olive."

Her back instantly went straight. "What is it?"

"Someone's been in here." He pointed to the zipper.

It was partially open. She was certain they'd closed it completely.

Jason's muscles stiffened as he turned toward her. "And whoever it was, I think they might still be inside."

Olive's hand moved instinctively toward the small knife hidden in her pocket.

The stakes were too high for them to be naive.

Whoever was inside their tent could be dangerous. Someone could be onto them and waiting to strike.

Jason nodded, signaling he was going to open the flap.

They both crouched as if it might contain a wild animal. Every sense was on high alert as they braced themselves for danger.

CHAPTER 29

Jason reached for the tent zipper, then stopped.

His hand hovered over the pull tab as he listened intently to the sounds from inside—soft rustling that could be someone going through their belongings.

Olive's pulse hammered in her throat as she imagined all the possibilities. One of Brad's security team searching for evidence. A local who'd decided festivalgoers made easy targets. Or worse—whoever had been responsible for the other disappearances, come to add two more names to their list.

Jason held up three fingers, then two.

On one, he acted.

But instead of unzipping the tent and rushing in, Jason called out, "I know you're in there. Come out now."

The rustling inside stopped abruptly.

For a heart-stopping moment, complete silence stretched.

Olive heard her own breathing, unnaturally loud, even over the rushing river in the background.

Every shadow seemed to shift and move in her peripheral vision.

Then a familiar voice came from inside, muffled by the tent fabric. "It's me. Don't freak out."

Olive's knees nearly buckled with relief, but Jason remained tense beside her.

They'd learned not to trust voices in the dark. Too many people in this place weren't who they seemed to be.

They exchanged glances, having a silent conversation about whether this could be a trap. Jason's expression was grim but determined as he carefully unzipped the tent entrance, moving slowly enough to react if whoever was inside proved hostile.

Inside, barely visible in the darkness, sat a familiar silhouette.

As Olive's eyes adjusted, she saw Tevin's distinctive profile. He sat cross-legged on Olive's sleeping bag, looking as if he'd been waiting for them for some time. But his posture was alert, ready to move quickly if necessary.

"Tevin . . ." Olive sighed, relief and irritation warring in her voice as the adrenaline slowly drained from her system. "You scared the snot out of me. You could have given us some warning."

"Sorry. Didn't want to risk calling out and attracting attention." Tevin's voice was barely above a whisper as he shifted to make room for them in the cramped space. "I've been monitoring radio chatter, and there are patrols making rounds every hour."

"We noticed," Jason muttered as he sat on his mattress, still facing Tevin.

Olive sat beside Tevin, the three of them forming a small circle.

"Where have you two been?" Tevin asked, pushing his glasses up higher on his nose. "I've been waiting here for over an hour, and I was starting to think something happened to you."

"Reconnaissance." Jason's voice still carried the edge of someone prepared for a fight.

They told him about the mine, about Brad's house, and everything else they'd learned.

"Now it's your turn. What's so urgent that you broke into our tent in the middle of the night?" Jason asked when they finished.

Tevin's expression grew even more serious in the dim light of the small battery powered lantern between them. "We've got bigger problems than I thought. Much bigger."

Olive swallowed hard.

She didn't like the sound of that.

Olive held her breath as she waited for Tevin to continue.

"First, Chloe did stay at the lodge," Tevin said. "I was able to look at their books. She was there for two nights, but I didn't see anything else helpful. The entire festival staff initially stayed at the lodge."

"Go on," Jason said.

"I overheard what Becca was telling you about the missing girl in Tennessee."

"What about it?" Olive asked.

"I was curious, so I hiked just outside of town. That newer house you mentioned? The one where Brad is staying? Turns out there's reception there. I managed to get through to Rex."

Olive's pulse quickened. "And?"

"Two things. First of all, he said he tried to call you before you reached the lodge, but reception was bad."

"Did he say what he wanted?"

"He found out about another disappearance in this area."

She sat up straighter. "Who?"

"A man named Hector Velasquez. He's from Mexico City and moved to this area for some job opportunity."

"Did he say what kind of job?" Jason asked.

Tevin shook his head. "No, just that it would be fast money that he wanted to send back to his family. One of his cousins is actually a lawyer in St. Louis. He heard about what happened and told the police. Otherwise, this guy would have probably just disappeared and never been heard about again."

"Do you have a picture?" Olive asked.

Tevin nodded and scrolled on his phone. A moment later, he showed them a picture of a Hispanic man, probably in his late twenties, who stood smiling with dusty mountains in the background.

But it was what was on his wrist that caught her attention.

It was a bracelet . . . one that looked an awful lot like the one she'd seen by the blood on the trail today.

CHAPTER 30

Olive showed them both the photo she'd taken on the trail.

None of them could deny the truth.

"The list of missing people is growing," Olive murmured.

"That's not all. The missing girl from Tennessee? Her name was Jessica Houser. Twenty-one years old. She did intern for Brad and this new exercise app he tried to launch." Tevin paused. "When her internship ended, she never returned home."

Jason leaned forward. "You sure? We did a background check on Brad."

"His name was buried in the paperwork. But it was there."

Another puzzle piece clicked into place in Olive's mind. "Just as we suspected, this isn't his first time running a fraudulent scheme—or failed business venture."

"These people are good at covering their tracks. Different company names, different financial structures, carefully laundered paper trails. Someone with serious resources is backing this operation."

Olive thought about the mansion they'd seen, about Brad's obvious love of money. "Question is, what's the real purpose of these businesses? Is Brad just a terrible entrepreneur? If so, why the pattern of disappearances?"

She tried to think like her dad. If he'd been involved with something like this, what would his motivation have been?

She wasn't sure.

"That's what we need to figure out. But there's something else." Tevin pulled out his phone. "Your signal problems aren't natural. Someone's using a signal blocking device. It creates the appearance of cell service while actually preventing any real communication."

"Why would they do that?" Olive was beginning to suspect she knew the answer.

"Same reason you jam communications in any tactical situation." Tevin's cheek twitched. "To prevent your targets from calling for help."

The implications settled over them like a cold blanket.

They weren't just dealing with festival fraud. They were dealing with something that required military-grade operational security. There had to be more to this.

"There's one more thing," Tevin continued. "About Becca Morrison."

"What about her?"

"She's not just researching festivals for school. The missing girl from Tennessee—Jessica Houser—was her roommate and best friend."

Olive's stomach dropped as she processed Tevin's words. "So Becca's here to—"

"To investigate what happened to her friend. And she has no idea how dangerous this situation really is." Tevin's expression was grave. "She's walking into the same trap that may have gotten Jessica either abducted or killed, and she doesn't even know it."

Olive thought about the young journalism student, limping around on her injured ankle, asking innocent questions about the festival's impact on rural communities. If Brad and his associates realize why she's really here . . .

"We have to protect her," Olive said.

"Agreed. But we also can't blow our own cover."

Jason ran a hand through his hair. "This is getting more complicated by the hour."

"And more dangerous," Tevin added. "Whatever happened to Chloe, Jessica, and the others, it's about to happen again. We just don't know when or who the target is."

Outside their tent, the festival grounds remained deceptively quiet. But Olive could feel the weight of hidden watchers and unknown threats pressing in from all sides.

They were running out of time to figure out what was really happening in Grayfall.

Chloe was missing, and every second counted.

She couldn't sit on the sidelines any longer.

It was time to get her hands dirty.

Just as that thought crossed her mind, gunfire split the air outside.

CHAPTER 31

Olive, Jason, and Tevin all darted from the tent, anxious to see what was happening. A quick check of her watch told her it was 2:30 a.m.

Others had also climbed from their tents, curious —and scared.

Everyone seemed to gravitate toward the Main Street area, questions murmuring through the air.

Olive tried to pick up on what had happened. Tried to listen to the conversations around her in case somebody knew something.

But everyone seemed clueless.

However, that gunfire had come from somewhere close.

And she'd be lying if she said she wasn't worried.

"It's okay, everyone." Max appeared in front of

them, waving his hands in the air to get their attention.

"What's going on?" Jason yelled. "Was someone hurt?"

"A few festivalgoers decided that they didn't want to stay any longer," Max explained. "So they ventured up the mountain, trying to get back to the lodge. Along the way they encountered a bear on the trail."

Gasps sounded around them.

"What happened then?" someone called.

"Thankfully, Tom saw them leaving and decided to trail behind them, just in case something like this were to happen," Max explained. "And it's a good thing that he did. When he saw the bear, he fired his gun in the air and the bear ran away. Everybody is safe and they're heading back here now."

Murmurs of relief followed.

"But I'd like to remind everybody that we are in the middle of a wilderness," Max continued. "This isn't Disney World. There are real dangers out there. And I encourage all of you to stay here and not try to leave on your own. Because if you do, there are no guarantees we can protect you."

Something about his words left a cold, hollow feeling in Olive's gut.

A few minutes later, everyone had scattered.

As Olive and Jason climbed into their tent, they exchanged a look.

Thunder rumbled in the distance, low and ominous. Through their tent's thin walls, she heard the wind picking up, rustling through the abandoned buildings of Grayfall with an almost mournful sound.

"There's a storm coming," Jason noted.

As if summoned by his words, the first fat raindrops began pattering against their tent.

Within minutes, the gentle patter had turned into a steady drumming. Shouts echoed across the festival grounds as people scrambled for shelter.

The earlier sounds of revelry turned to complaints and distress as the reality of spending a stormy night in cheap tents with no proper rain gear set in. People called to each other, footsteps splashed as people rushed through rapidly forming puddles, and the occasional curse cut through the air as someone tripped over tent stakes in the darkness.

"I guess we're settling back in for the night whether we want to or not," Jason said.

Olive lay back on her thin sleeping bag, staring at the tent ceiling as rain drummed overhead. Despite her body's exhaustion, her mind raced, planning and replanning their next moves.

Tomorrow, she needed to talk to Connor again.

She needed to find a way to access that promotional footage without arousing suspicion. Maya might have useful information too if Olive could catch her during a sober moment.

Most importantly, they needed to find a way to protect Becca without breaking their cover. The young journalism student was walking around with a target on her back, asking questions about Brad's prior businesses and completely unaware she was investigating the very people who might have done something to her best friend.

But what worried Olive most was a thought she couldn't shake: What happened when the other festivalgoers finally reached their breaking point?

The accommodations were terrible, the promised headliners no-shows, the food inadequate, and now they were trapped in a thunderstorm with equipment that clearly wasn't designed for actual camping.

Did Brad want everyone to be stranded here for a reason?

The question sent a chill down Olive's spine. She thought about the signal jamming, the security patrols, and the way the guides had positioned themselves earlier to prevent people from leaving.

Everything about this operation suggested careful planning and serious resources.

People who'd invested this much in . . . in whatever they were planning . . . didn't usually just let their victims walk away when things got inconvenient.

"Jason?" she whispered.

"Mmm?"

"What do you think happens tomorrow when people start demanding to leave?" She needed his opinion, needed to stop spinning the questions in her mind.

He was quiet for a long moment, and when he spoke, his voice carried the same unease she felt. "I think we're about to find out just how trapped we really are."

Outside, the storm intensified, and Olive couldn't shake the feeling that the weather was the least of their problems.

CHAPTER 32

Despite everything—the cramped quarters, the storm raging outside, the constant awareness of Jason's warm presence beside her—Olive eventually fell into an uneasy sleep.

Her dreams were filled with dark tunnels and watching eyes, voices calling for help from places she couldn't reach. She dreamed of Chloe running through the ruins of Grayfall, her coral pink silk catching on rusted metal as shadowy figures pursued her deeper into the mountains.

Thunder crashed overhead, jolting Olive partially awake.

The storm had intensified, and rain hammered against their tent with the force of a waterfall. As consciousness slowly returned, she became aware of something else—a cold, wet sensation against her cheek.

Drip.

Another drop of water hit her face, then another.

She fully opened her eyes.

Their tent was leaking, she realized. Water seeped through the cheap fabric and pooled on the floor around them.

"Oh no," she gasped, sitting up quickly.

The movement sent a splash of cold water across her sleeping bag.

Looking down, she saw that the entire floor of their tent was covered with several inches of water, and their belongings were floating like debris from a shipwreck.

"Jason!" She shook his shoulder urgently. "Jason, wake up!"

He jolted up straight. "What's wrong?"

"We're flooding." She gestured to the water surrounding them. "The whole tent is underwater."

Jason frowned as he seemed to feel the cold water soaking through his sleeping bag. "How fast is the water rising?"

"I don't know. I just woke up." Olive was already trying to salvage their gear, pulling her backpack out of the water. "My phone—"

"Is it waterproof?"

"Water resistant, but not waterproof." She

checked the device, relieved to find it still functioning despite being damp. "The photos from Elias's office are still there."

"The cloth swatch from the mine?"

She found it in her backpack. "I put it in a sealed bag, so it's fine."

"We can't stay here, Olive. This tent could be completely underwater soon."

The rain still pounded the tent. If anything, the storm seemed to be getting stronger.

"Where can we go?" she asked. "Every tent in the place is probably flooding."

Her question hung in the air a moment before chaos erupted all around them.

Through the thin walls, they heard other festivalgoers dealing with the same crisis—people calling out in distress, the sound of tent zippers being frantically opened and closed, splashing footsteps as campers tried to find higher ground or better shelter.

Jason pulled on his boots in the ankle-deep water. "The buildings. Some of those old structures might still have roofs that actually work."

"Or they might collapse on us."

"Better than drowning in our sleep."

Another thought hit Olive. "Do you think there's

any danger of flash flooding here? Do we need to warn others?"

Jason shook his head. "The conditions aren't right for it—not yet, at least. But we'll keep our eyes open. At the first sign people could be in danger because of the storm, we'll warn them."

"That sounds like a good plan."

Another flash of lightning illuminated their tent, followed by a crash of thunder that shook the ground beneath them.

In that brief moment of light, Olive saw the water level had risen even higher, nearly to the top of their mattresses, which were on the ground.

They were no longer camping—they were sitting in a small lake.

And Jason was right. They needed to get out of here before it was too late.

CHAPTER 33

Olive unzipped the tent and looked out at the blurry, rain-drenched darkness on the other side.

It was a soggy mess out there.

Some people had left their tents and were now dancing in the rain.

She spotted some flashlights and, from their position, assumed it was probably security keeping an eye on things.

"The free alcohol." Jason peeked out behind her. "Some people are probably passed out cold and don't realize they're sleeping in puddles. Others are getting soaked as they dance."

"I just hope no one does anything stupid."

"We need to find somewhere dry." Jason shouldered their soggy gear. "And higher up."

They stepped into the rain, carrying their backpacks, and the drops pelted them. Then they began to pick their way through the muddy campsite, past tents sagging under the weight of collected rainwater and others that had clearly taken on significant flooding. Most remained ominously quiet.

"There." Olive pointed toward the old church. "It's on higher ground. I wonder if we can get inside."

They headed that way. Jason tried the door, and it was unlocked.

Jason tested the floorboards before motioning for her to come inside.

As Olive and Jason stepped through the warped wooden doors, escaping the driving rain, they were immediately hit by the musty smell of rotting wood mixed with something sharper—the metallic tang of rusted metal and the sour odor of standing water that had pooled and stagnated in hidden corners.

Their flashlight beams revealed a space that had once been sacred but now felt haunted by neglect. The wooden pews sat in crooked rows, some collapsed entirely, their boards warped and split from years of moisture and temperature fluctuations. Hymnals lay scattered across the floor, their pages swollen and illegible, creating a carpet of molding paper that released the sweet, cloying smell of decomposition with each step.

The altar area was partially collapsed, the wooden platform tilted at a dangerous angle where the floor joists beneath had rotted through. Behind it, stained glass windows that had once depicted biblical scenes were now broken puzzles, with colored glass fragments scattered across the floor like discarded jewels.

Despite the decay, the space offered shelter from the storm raging outside, and they gratefully moved deeper into the ruins to escape the wind and rain that had been soaking them to the bone.

At once, memories from nearly a decade ago hit her.

Memories of her father's brief stint as a pastor at a small community church in Indiana. It was the place her family had moved after leaving Texas . . . and Jason.

She'd never quite understood why, after all the scams her father had pulled, he'd then decided to go into ministry. He'd never shown any interest in church before. She found the whole thing suspicious.

But she'd been coached by her parents on how to act like a good Christian girl. Every time the church doors had opened, she and her sisters had been there.

Though Olive had been apprehensive at first, she'd come to appreciate the people there and the community.

However, it was while her father served at that

church in Indiana that her entire family had been murdered.

Nausea began to roil inside her at the memories.

"This could be worse," Jason murmured, pulling her from her thoughts.

"Could it?" Olive frowned as she heard something scampering in the distance. A rat?

Jason pulled out some blankets from his pack—blankets that had somehow stayed dry. "At least we won't freeze."

"At least," she murmured.

But this was the first time she'd set foot in church since her family's murders . . . and she might not survive the ghosts coming back into the light.

Jason spread one blanket over the floor and held onto the other. They'd briefly considered settling on a pew, but the seats were narrow and hard—not very comfortable.

As they sat side by side on the narrow space, both still damp from their rescue efforts, Olive realized they were going to have to share body heat whether they wanted to or not.

"Come here." Jason lifted the edge of his blanket as he spread it out. "You're shivering."

She was, though she wasn't sure if it was from cold or nerves. But the invitation was practical, necessary even.

She scooted closer until they were sitting pressed together, the shared blanket wrapped around both of them. Thankfully, their clothes had remained fairly dry, protected by the sleeping bags covering them.

The warmth was immediate and comforting. Jason's solid presence beside her, the familiar scent of his skin, the way he automatically adjusted his position to make her more comfortable—it all felt so natural, so right, that for a moment she almost forgot why she'd been keeping her distance.

"Better?" he asked.

"Much." She leaned into his warmth, letting herself relax for the first time all day. "Thank you. For the blankets, for moving us, for . . . everything."

"We're partners," Jason said. "We take care of each other."

But the way he said it, the gentleness in his voice, suggested something deeper than professional courtesy. Her heart pounded harder.

They sat in comfortable silence for a while, listening to the storm outside. It was almost 4 a.m. They wouldn't be getting much sleep—morning would be here before they knew it.

It had been a long, long night.

"Just think," Olive started. "Brad and all his friends are warm and dry and probably drinking champagne while we're huddled in an abandoned building like refugees."

"If I had to guess, the party is probably still going strong over there."

"While his paying customers sleep in flooded tents." The injustice of it made her angry all over again.

"Do you remember," Jason's voice dropped to an intimate level, "that time we got caught in the rain at the football game?"

Olive smiled despite everything. "It was homecoming. The game was so intense that I sat through the entire fourth quarter in a downpour. But I couldn't take my eyes off you. You were the star quarterback who won the game and took the school to the state championship that year."

"I still remember you were wearing that blue sweater that you said was your lucky football game outfit."

"Which was completely ruined by the end of the night." She laughed softly. "I was so mad at myself for not bringing an umbrella."

"I did give you my letterman jacket even though you were already soaked through."

"Yes, and I appreciated that. But I felt so bad for you. You were soaked to the bone."

"Hey, I was trying to be chivalrous. And I was on an adrenaline high after winning the game."

The memory was sweet and painful at the same time.

They'd been so young then, so sure that what they had would last forever. So naive about how easily love could be destroyed by circumstances beyond their control.

"We were different people then." Olive's voice came out scratchy with emotion.

"Were we?" Jason's voice was thoughtful. "Sometimes I think we're exactly the same. Just . . . carrying more scars."

She turned to look at him. His face was serious, open in a way that made her heart ache with possibility and fear.

Sitting here with him, warm and safe despite their circumstances, sharing memories and gentle touches, felt like setting herself up for heartache all over again. She was falling back into the same patterns, the same feelings, the same dangerous hope that maybe this time would be different.

But maybe, just maybe, that was a risk worth taking.

Somewhere in these mountains, Chloe Kingston was still missing, Olive reminded herself. She still depended on them to find the truth.

But for now, in this small bubble of warmth and

memory, Olive let herself remember what it felt like to be loved by Jason Stewart. Even if it was only for one more night.

CHAPTER 34

ELEVEN YEARS AGO, BLUE RIDGE MOUNTAINS, GEORGIA

As Olive's family hiked with the Hendersons toward the first location marked on Dad's map, they all fell into a comfortable stride through the trees. Dad talked to Mr. Henderson and Michael up front. Mom stayed with the twins at the end.

And Olive found herself walking beside a very chatty Mrs. Henderson.

"Is this your first treasure hunt?" Mrs. Henderson asked, slightly breathless from the climb. She'd chosen cute hiking boots, and Olive noticed her wincing with each step on the rocky terrain.

"No, we've done several," Olive replied, the lie coming easier than it should have. She'd learned to weave truth into her father's fictional narratives, making them more believable. "Dad has a real talent for reading historical clues."

Her eyes brightened. "How exciting! And you've actually found things before?"

Olive glanced ahead to where Dad was regaling Mr. Henderson with stories of previous discoveries—silver coins from a Revolutionary War battlefield outside Savannah, jewelry buried by fleeing Confederate sympathizers near Atlanta, artifacts from forgotten settlements in the Appalachian foothills.

Each story was detailed, convincing, and probably completely fictional, but Dad told them with the passionate enthusiasm of a true historian.

She watched as he gestured animatedly, describing the painstaking research that had led to each discovery, the months of correspondence with university professors and local historical societies.

Mr. Henderson hung on every word, occasionally asking technical questions that Dad answered with impressive expertise.

"Sometimes," Olive chose her words carefully to avoid outright lies, "Dad says treasure hunting is part history, part detective work, and part luck."

"Your father certainly seems to know what he's doing," Mrs. Henderson observed, following Olive's gaze. "Michael is absolutely fascinated. He's been so bored lately—video games and social media don't seem to interest him anymore. But this . . . this is bringing out a curiosity I haven't seen in years."

Olive felt a stab of guilt watching the teenager's

animated face as he listened to her father's stories. Michael was asking intelligent questions about historical research methods, Civil War battle strategies, and artifact preservation.

For the first time since they'd met, he looked genuinely engaged with the world around him rather than retreating into his phone.

"How did your father first get interested in treasure hunting?" Mrs. Henderson continued.

"Family stories." Olive fell back on one of Dad's standard explanations. "His great-grandfather supposedly had some connection to the Civil War, and there were always legends about hidden family valuables. Dad started researching to see if any of it was true."

It wasn't entirely a lie. Dad expertly wove family history into his cons, making them more personal and believable. But Olive suspected his "great-grandfather" story was as fictional as Cornelius Slattery.

They reached a small clearing where an old stone foundation marked the remains of what Dad claimed was a Civil War-era homestead. The structure was real enough—probably the foundation of some long-forgotten mountain cabin—but Dad's historical interpretation was likely pure invention.

"This is it." Dad consulted his leather portfolio with the dramatic flair of a seasoned performer. "According to the historical records, this was the

Whitmore homestead. Jeremiah Whitmore was a Union sympathizer who helped runaway slaves reach the Underground Railroad routes through Tennessee."

Olive watched her father transform the simple stone foundation into a compelling piece of Civil War history, complete with details about the family who'd supposedly lived there, their political affiliations, and their connection to Cornelius Slattery's flight north.

He pulled out a professional-looking metal detector from his backpack and began sweeping the area with scientific precision.

"According to the map, Cornelius stopped here to rest his horses and resupply," Dad explained. "The riddle suggests he might have buried a small cache nearby as a test for anyone following his trail. Something to confirm they were on the right track before revealing the location of the main treasure."

The Hendersons watched with rapt attention as Dad methodically covered the clearing, explaining his technique and the historical logic behind his search pattern. Even the twins stood quietly as if sensing that something important was about to happen.

Despite her skepticism, Olive held her breath. Part of her—the part that was still fourteen and wanted to believe in magic—hoped that maybe this time Dad's stories might be real.

The metal detector began beeping near a cluster of old oak trees, the steady electronic pulse growing faster and more insistent as Dad moved closer to whatever was buried beneath the soil.

Dad's face lit up with what appeared to be genuine surprise as he knelt to examine the ground, though Olive noticed how his "surprise" was perfectly timed and expertly performed.

"Well, I'll be." He carefully brushed soil away from something metallic, his movements deliberate as he built suspense for his audience. "Look at this."

With the reverence of an archaeologist uncovering a priceless artifact, he pulled out what appeared to be an antique compass, tarnished with age but intact. The brass surface caught the dappled sunlight filtering through the oak leaves, and Olive could see initials engraved on its surface that matched the name on their treasure map: C.S.

Cornelius Slattery.

The Hendersons gasped in amazement while the twins clapped their hands in delight, bouncing on their toes with excitement. Even Mom looked impressed, though Olive caught the slight frown that suggested she was wondering when Dad had planted the compass—and how he'd managed to do it without anyone noticing.

"This is unbelievable." Mr. Henderson pulled out his phone to take pictures, his voice carrying the awe of someone witnessing a genuine historical discovery. "You're actually finding pieces of history. This could be in a museum!"

"The map was accurate," Dad said with satisfaction, holding the compass up to catch the light. "Which means we're on the right track for the main treasure site. Cornelius left this here as confirmation—a sign for anyone clever enough to follow his clues."

Olive watched the compass spin in Dad's palm, its needle seeking magnetic north just as it had over a century ago—if it was really that old. The craftsmanship looked authentic, the tarnishing seemed genuine, and the initials were worn in a way that suggested decades of handling.

But she'd learned not to underestimate her father's attention to detail when it came to his cons.

"Can I hold it?" Michael's voice was filled with wonder as he asked the question.

Dad handed over the compass with a smile, and Olive watched the teenager examine it with the reverence of someone touching actual history. His parents crowded around, marveling at the weight of the brass, the smoothness of the worn edges, the way the needle moved with their movements.

In that moment, watching their faces light up with excitement and wonder, Olive felt the full weight of what her father was doing.

This wasn't just about money—though she was sure that was coming.

It was about selling people a dream, a fantasy of adventure and discovery that made their ordinary lives feel magical.

And the terrible thing was, Olive could see why it worked. Standing in that forest clearing, holding what appeared to be a genuine Civil War-era artifact, even she felt the pull of possibility.

Maybe this time the treasure hunt was real. Maybe this time Dad's stories were true.

Maybe this time, she wouldn't have to watch him break good people's hearts.

But as Dad began explaining the next phase of their quest, Olive knew she was fooling herself.

The compass was just the opening move in a game that would end with the Hendersons poorer and her family on the run again.

The only question was: How much damage would be done before the final act played out?

CHAPTER 35

PRESENT DAY

Olive woke slowly, consciousness returning in gentle waves rather than the sharp alertness that usually marked her mornings. She felt surprisingly rested, warm and safe in a way that seemed impossible given their circumstances.

It took her a moment to realize why.

She was leaning against the wall, curled against Jason's chest, her head tucked under his chin, his arm wrapped securely around her waist. She could feel the steady rhythm of his breathing, the solid warmth of his body next to hers.

For just a moment, she let herself enjoy the feeling of being held, of being safe, of waking up next to someone who cared about her. It reminded her of when the world had been simpler, and love had felt like something she could keep.

Then reality crashed back.

The investigation. Their cover. The professional boundaries she'd carefully constructed between them.

Olive pulled away, perhaps more sharply than necessary.

Jason stirred but didn't wake. He merely shifted to accommodate her movement before settling back into sleep.

Pale morning light filtered through the cracks between the boards covering the windows. As the beams of light hit Jason's face, he somehow looked younger, more peaceful than she'd seen him since they'd arrived.

She forced herself to look away and quietly stood. The closeness, the shared memories, the feeling of connection . . . they'd done something to her heart that she couldn't let happen again. Those feelings were too dangerous, too distracting, too likely to compromise both her judgment and her mission.

Stepping outside, Olive stopped short at the scene that greeted her.

The festival grounds looked like a war zone.

Though a few tents had been on higher ground and still stood, the storm had left its mark on everything else. Collapsed tents lay scattered across the muddy ground like deflated balloons. Their contents spilled out and were trampled into the dirt. Camping chairs had been overturned and blown against buildings, creating small mountains of twisted metal and torn fabric.

Though the morning air was crisp and clean after the rain, carrying the scent of wet earth and pine, underneath it she detected something else.

The lingering smell of fear and desperation.

By the time Jason emerged from the church, other festivalgoers were beginning to stir, crawling out of their own damaged accommodations with expressions that ranged from hungover confusion to outright anger.

"What happened?" Maya's voice carried across the campsite, shrill with dismay. She stood beside her tent, which looked surprisingly unscathed. "This is a disaster!"

Connor was already out and about, documenting the destruction with his camera. He moved methodically through the wreckage while shaking his head.

Dr. Z crawled out from his tent, which had collapsed.

People began gravitating toward the catering tent, moving like zombies in search of salvation. Their faces were pale and drawn, hair disheveled, clothes wrinkled and damp.

The free alcohol from the night before had clearly taken its toll, and now they were dealing with hangovers on top of everything else.

"Coffee," someone groaned. "Please tell me there's coffee."

The catering tent had fared better than most of the camp, its professional-grade construction having weathered the storm with minimal damage. But as festivalgoers lined up at the service window, their expressions grew increasingly dismayed.

"What do you mean there's no coffee?" an older man demanded, his voice cracking with desperation. "How can you not have coffee?"

The harried worker behind the counter—the same one who'd announced they'd run out of food the day before—spread his hands helplessly. "The coffee machine got damaged in the storm. We're trying to fix it, but . . ."

"This is unacceptable!" Maya pushed to the front of the line. "People paid thousands of dollars for this experience, and you can't even provide basic caffeine?"

"We've got granola bars." The worker held up a box of the generic breakfast bars.

A collective groan rose from the crowd.

A mix of sympathy and relief rushed through Olive—sympathy for people who'd been genuinely deceived, and relief that her coffee allergy meant she wasn't facing the same withdrawal symptoms as everyone else. She'd never been more grateful for her body's inability to process caffeine.

"I want to speak to whoever's in charge of this disaster!" someone called out. "Where's Brad?"

"He's . . . dealing with storm damage assessment," the catering worker said, though his tone suggested he had no idea where Brad actually was.

Jason appeared beside Olive, calmly surveying the chaos. "This is catastrophic."

As people reluctantly accepted their granola bar breakfast and wandered away grumbling, Olive scanned the crowd for familiar faces.

She spotted Connor, still documenting everything. Dr. Z, methodically eating his granola bar while reviewing something on his tablet. Tevin, maintaining his distance but clearly observing the crowd.

She would love more than anything to be able to go and sit beside him. To catch up over some Chinese food.

He was one in a million, and she hated that she had to keep her distance from him on this assignment.

But one face was notably absent.

"Have you seen Becca?" Olive tried to keep the concern out of her voice as she leaned toward Jason.

His expression sharpened as he scanned the

crowd. "No. And given what Tevin told us about why she's really here . . ."

They exchanged worried glances.

A young journalism student investigating her best friend's disappearance, alone in a place where people routinely vanished, after a night when someone had clearly been searching through the camp?

Not good.

"We need to find her." Olive abandoned any pretense of casual interest. "Now."

Because Olive's gut was telling her something was majorly wrong.

CHAPTER 36

As the grumbling crowd grew more restless around the catering tent, Brad Kellerman appeared like a man stepping out of a luxury spa rather than someone who'd supposedly weathered the same storm as everyone else.

His hair was perfectly styled, his designer outdoor attire looked freshly pressed, and he carried himself with the confident energy of someone who'd enjoyed a full night's sleep in comfortable, climate-controlled accommodations.

The contrast between his polished appearance and the bedraggled festivalgoers was so stark it felt almost insulting.

"Good morning, everyone!" Brad called out with theatrical enthusiasm, climbing onto a table to address the crowd. "I know last night was challenging, but that's what makes this such an authentic wilderness experience!"

A chorus of disbelieving mutters rose from the assembled festivalgoers, but Brad pressed on with his practiced showman's smile.

"Don't you all worry—I'm going to have my crew help clean up from the storm. Your tents and sleeping bags should all be dry by tonight."

More muttering.

"I have some exciting updates about today's schedule." He pulled out a tablet that looked suspiciously unaffected by the supposed communication difficulties everyone else was experiencing. "While we've had some last-minute changes to our lineup—"

"You mean more cancelations?" Frat Boy interrupted, his hangover making him even less diplomatic than usual.

"Some of our originally scheduled acts have encountered some difficulties," Brad said. "But we've arranged for even more incredible local talent to fill those slots. And the best news is, we're expecting a new group of festivalgoers—people who bought the two-day pass—to arrive any time now. The energy level is going to be electric!"

"We already don't have enough food!" someone yelled.

"We have more coming." Brad checked his watch. "It should be arriving any time."

"How many more people are supposed to come?" someone called out.

"Only about fifty," Brad answered.

More questions came from the crowd:

"Do they know all the bands have canceled?"

"Is Obscurity still coming?"

"We deserve a refund!"

"Our logistics team is working on all of these details," Brad said as he scanned the crowd. "Please trust me when I say everything is under control."

As Brad continued his damage control, Olive glanced at Connor, who recorded everything with his camera.

"We need to talk to him," she whispered to Jason.

He nodded.

As the crowd began to disperse, she and Jason casually drifted toward where Connor now packed his equipment. But first, Tevin caught their gaze and gave them a nod, letting them know he was keeping an eye on things as well.

"That was quite a performance," Olive started, maintaining her cover as a concerned festivalgoer.

"You can say that again," Connor muttered.

"I'm sure you've seen a lot since you were charged with documenting this fiasco," Jason said.

"You have no idea." He snorted.

"To be honest, it's not the food, the broken promises, or the accommodations that have me worried. This whole place is starting to feel . . . dangerous."

Connor glanced around as if to make sure they weren't being overheard, then leaned closer. "You and me both. I'm starting to think we're in serious trouble here. The way Brad's talking, the condition of this place, the fact that people keep . . . disappearing."

"Disappearing?" Jason played innocent.

Connor frowned. "I haven't seen Becca yet today. She was supposed to meet with me so she could ask some questions about my experiences as a videographer at these types of things. When she didn't show up, I checked her tent, and it was empty, but she wasn't at breakfast."

"That doesn't sound good," Olive murmured.

"And with everything Chloe told me before she disappeared . . ." Connor stopped himself, realizing he was about to reveal more than he'd intended.

Her lungs froze. "Chloe told you things before she disappeared? What kind of things?"

Connor's expression grew even more troubled. "I'm saying too much."

"But are you?" Olive stepped closer. "If there's something going on here and people are in danger, then we need to get to the bottom of it—before anyone else 'disappears.'"

Connor remained quiet for a long moment, his gaze moving between their faces as if trying to assess whether he could trust them. Finally, he seemed to reach a decision.

"Look, I don't know who you two really are," he started. "But you seem like you actually care about what's happening to people here. Most of these folks are just worried about getting their money back."

Olive's pulse quickened. How much should they say?

"I'm just a contractor trying to make sure my wife has a good time," Jason said. "And a concerned citizen and Army vet."

"Right." Connor's expression was skeptical but not hostile. "Look, I don't care who you are. In fact, maybe it's better if I don't know. But if you're genuinely worried about Chloe and Becca, maybe we need to work together."

Connor looked around nervously before continuing, his voice dropping even lower. "I might be able to help, but it would mean taking a serious risk."

Olive's pulse spiked. "What kind of risk?"

"I have hours of footage from the promotional shoot. Behind-the-scenes stuff, conversations, things that didn't make it into the final video." Connor's hands fidgeted with his camera strap. "I can't help but wonder if there's something on those recordings that shows why Chloe got so upset and left. Maybe something that could explain what happened to her."

Jason leaned forward. "You'd be willing to share that footage?"

"I should absolutely *not* share that footage," Connor said with a bitter laugh. "I'm sure there's a clause somewhere in my contract that says I'll be sued into oblivion if I show it to anyone without authorization. Brad was very specific about confidentiality when he hired me."

Connor paused, watching as Brad continued working the crowd in the distance, his smile never wavering despite the obvious hostility of his audience.

"But if it means helping Chloe or Becca . . ." Connor's voice trailed off, then hardened with resolve. "Who cares about the contract? People's lives are more important than my legal liability."

"What do you need from us?" Olive asked.

"Discretion. Absolute discretion." Connor glanced around again, noting the positions of the security team members who were stationed throughout the crowd. "We'll need to be very careful about this. If Brad or his people find out what I'm showing you . . ."

"We understand," Jason said. "How do you want to do this?"

Connor appeared to consider their options, weighing risks against potential benefits. "Give me about ten minutes to get back to my tent and set up the equipment. It's the large blue one on the far side of the camp. Number forty-three on the stakes."

"Got it," Jason said.

"Take different routes to get there, and don't arrive together. Make it look like you're just wandering around assessing storm damage or something." Connor's voice carried the nervous energy of someone who knew he was about to cross a line he couldn't uncross. "And whatever you do, don't let anyone see you going into my tent. If we're being watched—which I'm pretty sure we are—this could get very dangerous very quickly."

Olive's chill had nothing to do with the morning air. "Dangerous how?"

Connor's expression was grim as he looked toward Brad, who was now surrounded by a small group of security personnel who surveyed the crowd.

"Let's just say I don't think we're the first people to ask too many questions about what really happened to them," Connor finally said.

With that ominous warning, Connor shouldered his equipment and walked away, leaving Olive and Jason to contemplate just how deep they were willing to go into a situation that was looking more dangerous by the hour.

CHAPTER 37

Olive and Jason made their way to Connor's tent through different routes, using the storm damage as cover for their wandering.

Olive pretended to search for salvageable belongings from destroyed campsites, while Jason appeared to be helping other festivalgoers assess their damaged gear.

Connor's tent was larger and more professional than most of the others—clearly designed for someone who needed to store expensive equipment. When they slipped inside one by one, they found him hunched over a laptop with several external hard drives connected, his face illuminated by the blue glow of the screen. Olive wasn't sure how much longer those electronics would last without being charged, but she hoped it was long enough to find some evidence.

"Any trouble getting here?" Connor barely looked up from his work as he asked the question.

"All clear." Jason settled onto one of the equipment cases Connor had arranged as makeshift seating.

"Good. I've been going through the footage since I got back to my tent, and . . ." Connor's expression was troubled as he turned the laptop toward them. "There's definitely something here you need to see."

The screen showed behind-the-scenes footage from the promotional shoot, time-stamped three weeks earlier. The video quality was professional, capturing details that the official promotional material had carefully edited out.

"This is from the second day of filming." Connor clicked to a specific timestamp. "Watch Chloe's face during this conversation."

On screen, Chloe appeared vibrant and enthusiastic. But as the footage continued, Olive saw the subtle changes in her demeanor. Her bright smile became more forced, her body language grew tense, and she kept glancing nervously toward people off-camera.

"Now here's where it gets interesting." Connor advanced to another section. "This is Brad talking to some of his financial backers. They thought the cameras were off."

The audio was partially muffled, but they could hear fragments of conversation. "Kingston's daughter . . . family connections . . . liquidate assets if necessary."

Olive's blood ran cold. "That makes me wonder if someone was specifically targeting Chloe because of her father's wealth and connections."

"It gets worse," Connor said. "Watch this part."

The footage showed Chloe being introduced to several men in expensive suits—people who definitely weren't part of the festival crew. One of them made a comment that wasn't picked up clearly by the microphone, but Chloe's reaction was immediate and visceral.

Her face went pale, and she took several steps backward.

"What did he say to her?" Jason asked.

"I've been trying to enhance the audio, but I can't quite make it out. Something about her father's business dealings and how 'cooperation' would be in everyone's best interests." Connor's fingers clenched into fists. "After that conversation, Chloe left."

"And now she's missing," Olive murmured, more pieces falling into place.

Connor was about to respond when shouting erupted from outside the tent.

All three of them froze, listening as multiple voices carried across the campsite.

"Welcome to Grayfall Festival!" came Brad's familiar voice, though it sounded more strained than usual.

"What is this?" someone yelled. "This isn't what you advertised!"

"I know the accommodations aren't quite what you expected—"

"Accommodations? These are ruins! And why is everything flooded?"

Connor carefully lifted the edge of his tent flap, peering out toward the commotion. "New arrivals . . . or should I say, potential victims."

CHAPTER 38

Olive and Jason crowded behind Connor to get a view of the scene unfolding near the festival entrance.

A group of about thirty people stood staring in horror at the destroyed camping area, the ruins of Grayfall, and the inadequate facilities that bore no resemblance to the luxury experience they'd been promised.

Basically, it was the same song and dance as yesterday.

"It appears the shuttle's working again," Jason observed. "I don't know how they would have gotten here this early otherwise."

He had a good point.

The shock and anger of the newcomers was palpable even from a distance.

"This is a scam!" one woman shouted. "I'm calling the police!"

"I'm afraid cell service is quite limited out here," Brad said with practiced calm. "But I assure you, once you see what we have planned—"

The woman pulled out her cell phone and tried to dial.

"Lady, there's no cell service," came a voice from one of the existing festivalgoers. "We've been trying to call out since yesterday."

That was when Olive saw him.

Standing slightly apart from the main group of new arrivals, surveying the scene with calculating eyes, was a tall man with aristocratic features and blond hair. He wore expensive clothing that looked both outdoorsy and elegant. Everything about his posture suggested someone accustomed to getting his way.

Olive gasped. "That's him."

"Who?" Connor asked.

"Tristan Pembroke." Jason clearly recognized him from their research files. "Chloe's ex-boyfriend. The one who was cheating on her."

"What is he doing here?" Connor's voice carried a mixture of confusion and suspicion.

They watched as Tristan moved through the crowd with practiced ease, his attention focused not on Brad's damage control performance but on the faces of the existing festival attendees.

He was searching for someone—and Olive had a sinking feeling she knew who.

"He's looking for Chloe," she said. "Question is, why? And how did he know to come here?"

"Maybe he's working with Brad," Jason suggested. "Part of the setup."

"Or maybe he figured out she was in trouble and came to help." Connor's tone suggested he didn't really believe it.

As they watched, Tristan's gaze swept across the campsite. When his eyes passed over Connor's tent, Olive instinctively pulled back from the opening, though she was fairly certain he couldn't see them.

"If Tristan's here, either the situation is about to get a lot more complicated, or we're about to find out just how deep this conspiracy really goes," she murmured.

Outside, the new arrivals were becoming increasingly agitated. Their demands for refunds grew louder and more insistent. But security was already moving to contain the situation, herding people toward the "temporary shelter areas" while promising that everything would be explained shortly.

And through it all, Tristan Pembroke stood watching.

CHAPTER 39

Tristan Pembroke may have looked like he'd stepped off the cover of a men's fashion magazine, but right now his confidence was cracking around the edges.

Olive and Jason watched from Connor's tent as Sorrel led Tristan toward a tent on the far side of the camp. Even from a distance, the tension in Tristan's posture was obvious. His eyes kept scanning the ruins of Grayfall.

"We need to talk to him," Olive said as she watched him from the tent. "Before Brad's people get to him first."

"Agreed. But we need to be smart about this," Jason said. "If he's working with them—"

"Then we'll find out quickly enough."

They waited until Sorrel had left Tristan at his

assigned tent before slipping out of Connor's tent and making their move. Using the scattered debris and ruined buildings as cover, they crossed the campsite, timing their approach for when security was focused on the newest arrivals' continuing complaints.

Tristan had just ducked inside his tent when they reached it.

Without ceremony, Olive unzipped the entrance and stepped inside, Jason close behind her.

It was time to find out some answers.

Tristan spun around, his aristocratic composure dissolving into something much more vulnerable.

Up close, his movie-star good looks couldn't hide the dark circles under his eyes, the slight tremor in his hands, and the way his expensive outdoor gear hung loose on his frame as if he'd lost weight recently.

"Who are you?" he demanded. But his voice carried more fear than authority as he stood there with wide eyes and fisted hands.

"People who want to find Chloe." Olive stood blocking Tristan's only exit. "Same as you."

Tristan's defensive posture instantly crumbled, and he sank onto his mattress with the deflated air of someone who'd been carrying a terrible burden alone.

"You know about Chloe?" His accent was pure upper-class British, but stress had stripped away any arrogance. "Have you seen her . . . ? Is she . . . ?"

"She's missing." Jason sat on the other end of the mattress as he studied Tristan's reaction. "Question is, what do you know about it?"

Olive stood across from them but still near the bed.

Tristan ran his hands through his hair, destroying its magazine-worthy arrangement. "I came here looking for her. I know how stupid that sounds, especially after . . . after what I did. But I realized what an absolute loser I'd been, and I wanted to make things right."

"What changed your mind?" Olive settled onto an equipment case to make the conversation feel less confrontational.

"Everything." Tristan's voice sounded raw with regret. "Losing her made me realize she was the only real thing in my life. All the parties, the other women, the whole lifestyle—it's all meaningless."

"Keep going," Olive crossed her arms.

He pulled out his phone, scrolling to their text conversation. "She actually seemed open to talking when I first reached out. We had several good conversations, and she said she was ready to forgive me, ready to start fresh after this festival was over."

"But then she stopped responding," Jason guessed.

Tristan's expression drooped. "Completely. At first, I thought she was just busy or having second thoughts about giving me another chance. Then I started calling our mutual friends, and none of them had heard from her either." Tristan's hands shook slightly as he held his phone. "That's when I knew something was really wrong."

"So you came here," Olive finished. She could only guess that Chloe discovered she was able to text if she got close to that house where Brad was staying. Maybe, as part of the planning team, she'd even stayed in the house.

"I hired investigators, tracked down information about this festival, and pulled strings to get a last-minute spot." Tristan looked around the pathetic tent with disgust. "Though I clearly didn't do enough research about what I was walking into."

"You didn't come here for luxury," Olive reminded him.

His jaw hardened. "No, I came here to find Chloe."

CHAPTER 40

"You said Chloe seemed ready to start fresh after the festival was over," Jason said. "Did she say anything specific about what was happening here?"

Tristan nodded. "That's what made me really worried. Chloe can be . . . flighty. It would be absolutely like her to get bored with something and just take off for Bali or Morocco without telling anyone."

"Keep going," Jason said.

Tristan's expression grew more troubled. "Her last few texts made it seem like something was genuinely wrong. She said she was ready to have this whole thing over with, but that contractually she needed to wait until after the festival, which she predicted would be 'a complete disaster.'"

That would be an understatement . . . Olive mused. "Anything else?"

"She kept saying that things weren't like they seemed. That the people running this weren't who they pretended to be." Tristan showed them his phone screen. "Look at this one from three days before she disappeared."

Olive read the text aloud. "'I can't wait to get out of here. This whole thing feels wrong, and I'm starting to think I made a terrible mistake getting involved."

Tristan's aristocratic features hardened with anger. "I should have realized something was off about that."

"Did she ever mention anything about trees?" Olive remembered Chloe's final cryptic message. "Something about trees watching?"

Tristan went very still, his face pale. "Actually . . . yes, she did. And that's when I really started to worry."

Olive waited for Tristan to continue, her mind racing through possibilities.

"In one of our last conversations, Chloe mentioned feeling like she was being watched all the time," Tristan continued. "She said it was like 'the trees have eyes' and that she couldn't shake the feeling that people were monitoring her every move."

"People were watching her?" Jason leaned forward, his biceps flexing.

Olive's throat went dry at the sight of his muscles, and she looked away She couldn't afford to be distracted right now.

"She said the festival organizers had cameras everywhere, supposedly for promotional footage and security, but it felt excessive. Like surveillance rather than documentation." Tristan's voice dropped to a whisper. "She joked that she felt like she was the subject in some kind of nature documentary, but . . . I don't think she was really joking."

A few more pieces clicked into place in Olive's mind. The constant filming, the isolated location . . . it all suggested something much deeper than a con.

"Tristan, we think Chloe might have discovered something about this operation that made her dangerous to them. If that's true—" Before Olive could finish her thought, music erupted from outside the tent, accompanied by the crackle of a PA system coming to life.

"Ladies and gentlemen!" Brad's voice boomed across the campsite. "Please gather around the main stage for this afternoon's special performance! You won't want to miss this incredible opportunity to experience authentic Appalachian music culture!"

Through the tent walls, they heard people reluctantly moving toward the stage, grumbling but complying.

"We need to get out there." Olive rose from her makeshift seat. "But Tristan, if you really want to help find Chloe, you need to let us do the investigating."

"Why?" Tristan asked, though he was already moving toward the tent entrance. "Who are you people?"

Olive and Jason exchanged glances. Their cover was already compromised with Connor, and now they needed Tristan's cooperation if they were going to find Chloe before it was too late.

"We're professional investigators," Jason said. "And this situation may be far more dangerous than anyone anticipated."

CHAPTER 41

Olive, Jason, and Tristan exited the tent one by one.

Once out, they all gravitated toward the crowd near the stage where a band was setting up. Tristan gave them a look before branching away from them.

When Olive and Jason were alone, she leaned closer to him and whispered, "We need to get into that house where Brad is staying. If Chloe's being held anywhere or if there's evidence about what really happened to her, it could be inside."

"I agree, but it's too risky during the day," Jason argued. "That place is probably crawling with security, and if they catch us—"

"The house is our best shot at finding real evidence." Olive's mind raced through possibilities.

"This might be our best opportunity. I can go. Alone. It will be too obvious if both of us are gone."

A shadow of disapproval passed over his gaze. "Olive, if something goes wrong, I have no way to contact you. No way to help if—"

Before Jason could finish his thought, a commotion erupted near the stage.

The same weathered mountain man who'd warned them on the trail had somehow appeared in the center of the festival grounds, his presence causing festivalgoers to scatter in surprise and confusion.

"Y'all still here?" The Grayfall Guardian's voice carried across the valley with surprising authority as he climbed onto the stage platform. "Still playin' along with this here charade?"

"Sir, you need to leave immediately," one of the guards called out.

The old man ignored him. "Told y'all yesterday there's things in these hills that don't belong. Things that take what they want and leave nothin' but questions behind."

His gaze swept across the assembled crowd with the intensity of someone delivering a prophecy. Olive held her breath as she waited to hear what he had to say.

"But you didn't listen," he continued. "None of y'all ever listen. And now you're gonna pay!"

Olive's lungs tightened at his ominous words.

Even worse—she feared the man might be right.

Brad appeared from somewhere in the crowd, his face flushed with anger and embarrassment. "Security! Get this man off my stage!"

"Your stage?" The Guardian's laugh was bitter. "Boy, this here land belonged to my kin long before you set foot. And it'll be ours long after you're gone."

The guards were closing in now, but the old man wasn't finished.

"The roots run deep in Grayfall." His voice rose above the approaching footsteps. "Deep enough to hide secrets. Deep enough to swallow folks whole. Y'all best remember that."

As security finally reached him, the Guardian allowed himself to be escorted away.

"This is my cue," Olive whispered to Jason. "Everyone's watching the drama. I'm going now. I'll be careful."

Concern filled his gaze as he realized what she was talking about. "Olive, wait—"

But she had already slipped away from the crowd, using the chaos and confusion to disappear into the shadows between the abandoned buildings.

Behind her, Brad tried to regain control of his

audience, his voice strained with the effort of maintaining his cheerful facade.

This was Olive's chance. She couldn't blow it.

CHAPTER 42

From Olive's hiding spot behind an old gas station, she studied the house where Brad was staying, noting the layout, the windows, the potential entry points.

She'd had just enough time to go back to the tent. She'd changed her shoes, grabbed a black hat and a black hoodie. She'd slipped them on only once she was in the woods.

She counted at least two figures moving around inside—dark silhouettes visible through the large windows. Both appeared to be in what looked like a living area on the first floor. The back of the house faced the forest, providing cover for approach but also eliminating her ability to see if there were additional occupants.

This is insane, she told herself. *Breaking into a house*

with unknown hostiles inside, no backup, no communication.

But if there was even a chance that Chloe or Becca were being held inside . . .

Olive waited another five minutes, timing the movements of the figures and noting their patterns.

The people on the first floor now seemed to be stationary—probably watching television or working at a computer.

The back door was her best option. It faced away from the festival grounds and was partially concealed by an expensive-looking deck with outdoor furniture that would provide additional cover.

That was how she'd get inside.

Her muscles tensed as she readied herself to move.

Moving through the trees, Olive approached the house from the rear.

Her heart hammered against her ribs as she crossed the open ground between the forest and the building, expecting shouts or alarm bells at any moment.

The back door was locked, but it was a standard

residential deadbolt—nothing she couldn't pick. Her dad had taught her that skill.

Within thirty seconds, the mechanism clicked, disengaging.

She slipped inside and found herself in a mudroom that connected to the kitchen.

The contrast between this space and the festival conditions was jarring. It had granite countertops, stainless steel appliances, and even fresh flowers in expensive vases.

This was where the festival money had really gone. But why? Why pour money into a house at this location? It wasn't prime vacation property.

Voices drifted from the front of the house—two men discussing something in low tones in what appeared to be the living room.

Olive caught fragments, something about "schedules," "the next group," and "containment protocols."

She moved toward a staircase, her shoes silent on the hardwood floors. If there was evidence to be found, it would likely be in an office or study—somewhere Brad conducted business. She needed to start upstairs. Downstairs was too risky.

The first room at the top of the stairs was clearly a primary bedroom, expensively furnished but empty. The second was a guest room, also vacant. The third door opened into a bathroom that looked like it belonged in a luxury spa.

But the fourth door revealed exactly what she'd been hoping for—a bedroom with an office space in the corner. There was a large desk, filing cabinets, and multiple computer monitors that displayed what appeared to be security feeds from around the festival grounds.

Olive slipped inside and quietly closed the door behind her.

She needed to start searching.

But before she even made it to the desk, footsteps sounded on the stairs.

Heavy footsteps. Climbing steadily toward the second floor.

Panic raced through her.

She looked around for a hiding spot or alternative exit, but she only saw one door.

The footsteps came closer, accompanied by, "I just need to grab something."

Olive pressed herself against the wall behind the door, praying she wouldn't be found.

But as the footsteps paused right outside her door, she realized she might have just walked into the very trap she'd been trying to avoid.

CHAPTER 43

Olive's heart hammered so loudly in her ears she was certain whoever was approaching would hear it through the door.

She heard the soft sound of a hand touching the door handle.

Her mind raced. She frantically glanced around.

That was when she saw a closet door, partially obscured by a fake tree.

She darted toward it, slipping inside just as the office door opened. The closet was deeper than she'd expected, and she pressed herself behind some hanging coats and jackets.

Through the slightly opened closet door, she watched as someone entered the office.

Elias Mercer.

The lodge owner looked nothing like the cheerful

host he played for the festival guests. His face was drawn with stress, his usually perfect appearance disheveled, and his hands shook as he pulled out his phone.

What's he doing here? Olive wondered.

She'd assumed this was Brad's private residence, but Elias clearly had access and familiarity with the space.

Plus, how had he gotten here? Had he hiked in?

She hadn't seen or heard any helicopters recently.

Elias paced to the desk, his phone pressed to his ear as he waited for someone to answer. When the call connected, his voice was strained with barely controlled panic.

"Listen, we need to talk," he said without preamble. "This whole thing is spiraling out of control. Now that journalist girl is missing—"

A voice erupted from the phone, loud enough that Olive could hear the anger even if she couldn't make out specific words.

Elias held the device away from his ear, wincing at the volume.

"I know what the plan was," Elias said when the shouting subsided. "But it's not working. Nothing is going according to schedule."

More angry words from the other end. Elias's face grew paler with each exchange.

"I can't do this anymore." His voice cracked. "We

need to pull the plug. End it now before someone gets seriously hurt. Or before law enforcement shows up asking questions we can't answer."

Olive's throat tightened.

What in the world was he talking about?

From her hiding spot, Olive watched as Elias stepped back from the phone as if the person on the other end could reach through and strike him.

"I understand the financial implications," Elias said. "But if this goes wrong—if people start dying—"

The voice cut him off with what sounded like threats, and Elias's face went from pale to gray.

"Fine," he finally said. "Fine. But I want it on record that I advised against continuing. When this blows up, I don't want to be the only one taking the fall."

He ended the call and stood there for a moment, staring at his phone with the expression of a man who'd just signed his own death warrant. Then he pocketed the device and left the office, his footsteps heavy with defeat.

Olive remained hidden until she was certain he was gone.

Her mind raced with what she'd overheard.

Just as she suspected, Elias wasn't just the lodge owner—he was somehow involved in whatever was happening here.

And he was getting cold feet about something that involved people potentially dying.

She didn't like the sound of that.

CHAPTER 44

When the house had been quiet for several minutes, Olive emerged from the closet and moved quickly to the desk.

Someone else might return at any moment, and she needed to find evidence of what was really happening here.

From her position in the room, she could hear the band beginning to play. She may have even heard some boos from the audience.

She turned back to the desk. It was organized with file folders arranged alphabetically, computer screens displaying various security feeds and data charts, and a stack of documents marked with official-looking seals and classifications.

She pulled out her phone, grateful that she'd thought to bring a portable charger. Her battery was still at nearly full capacity, allowing her to photograph whatever evidence she could find.

The first folder was labeled "Logistics—Phase 3" and contained what appeared to be a list of employees. Olive didn't recognize any of the names. The second was marked "Financial Projections" and showed revenue streams that didn't match anything resembling a legitimate music festival. The amounts were in the millions.

Another folder contained what appeared to be a geological survey.

Why would they need a geological survey?

Olive photographed page after page, her hands growing steadier as her training took over despite her shock at what she was seeing.

There was definitely more going on here than met the eye.

Her hands trembled slightly as she continued photographing. Each image revealed another layer of the conspiracy. Financial records showing millions of dollars. Environmental impact reports. Shipping manifests.

She was photographing a page near the end of the stack when she heard it: the soft click of the door handle turning.

Panic shot through her system like ice water.

Someone was back.

She ducked under the desk, knowing the files were still out.

If this was Elias or Brad, they would know things hadn't been left this way.

Someone stepped inside.

She heard breathing, sensed a presence filling the doorway.

The footsteps paused.

Had this person seen her? Was he or she reaching for a weapon? Calling for security?

The footsteps moved closer.

And she realized this was the moment of truth.

Time was up.

CHAPTER 45

Olive's heart thundered so violently she was certain it would give her away.

The space beneath the desk was cramped and uncomfortable, forcing her to curl into a tight ball. At least the desk chair provided some concealment.

Footsteps crossed the hardwood floor with familiar precision.

They paused near the desk.

Her heart pounded even harder.

Whoever was in the room moved with the quick efficiency of someone retrieving something specific. Above her, papers rustled, and she heard the soft sound of a folder being lifted from the desk surface.

Olive pressed herself farther into the shadows under the desk, hardly daring to breathe.

After what felt like an eternity, the footsteps moved toward the door. It opened and closed, followed by the receding sound of someone heading back downstairs.

Olive remained frozen for several more minutes, waiting to make sure this person wasn't coming back.

When the house seemed quiet again, she carefully emerged from her hiding spot, her muscles protesting from the cramped position.

The folder she'd been photographing was gone, but she'd managed to document all but the last page. Still, she couldn't shake the feeling that she'd missed something crucial—something that might have been on that final page.

She quickly scanned the remaining materials on the desk, looking for anything else that might be useful. She saw nothing.

Now she needed to plan her exit strategy.

She needed to get out of the house without being detected.

As she rose, she glanced out the window.

Her breath caught.

What was that?

From this angle, she could see the other side of the mountain.

White tents had been set up there—a whole army of them.

There were too many for that to be where the staff was staying. And if it wasn't from this angle and her second-story position, she would have never seen those tents.

She stepped closer.

It was more than just tents.

There were two other buildings over there. They'd been painted an olive-green color and nearly blended in with the trees.

What in the world was going on here?

Making her way carefully toward the stairs, Olive paused at the top to listen for voices from below. The house seemed quiet, but she could see light coming from what appeared to be a living room area.

She descended slowly, testing each step to avoid creaking. Her shoes were graciously silent on the hardwood.

As she reached the bottom of the stairs, voices became audible from the front room.

Two men were engaged in what sounded like a heated discussion.

Moving carefully toward the kitchen and her planned exit route, Olive paused when she recognized one of the voices. Max—the muscle-bound security guard with the aggressive attitude and expensive hiking boots.

"I'm telling you, the timeline's too aggressive." Max's voice carried the frustrated tone of someone arguing a losing battle. "We're not ready for Phase Three."

"Orders came from the top," replied another voice—one Olive didn't immediately recognize. "The parameters have to be maintained regardless of readiness levels."

Olive crept closer to the living room entrance, hoping to get a better view of who Max was talking to and to hear more of their conversation. The hallway provided some cover, allowing her to position herself where she could see into the room without being immediately visible.

Max stood with his back to her, his bulky frame tense with agitation. Across from him sat a thin man in his fifties with silver hair and an expensive suit—definitely not festival staff. He looked like government or corporate management, someone who made decisions from behind a desk rather than implementing them in the field.

"I don't know how you think this is going to work," Max continued. "People are asking questions. They want to leave."

"We need to keep them here," the silver-haired man replied dismissively. "Do whatever it takes."

Olive leaned forward slightly, trying to get a better angle to photograph the unknown man.

If he was running this operation, his identity could be crucial evidence.

But as she shifted her weight, the old floorboard beneath her feet let out a loud creak.

CHAPTER 46

Both men stopped talking immediately.

"What was that?" the silver-haired man snapped.

Max was already moving toward the hallway, his hand reaching for something at his belt—probably a weapon. "Sounded like it came from the stairs."

Olive's mind raced through her options.

The back door was still her best exit route, but reaching it required crossing Max's line of sight.

The front door was closer but would put her in direct view of both men.

And hiding was no longer an option—they were actively searching for the source of the noise.

"Check upstairs," the silver-haired man ordered. "I'll search down here."

As Max's heavy footsteps headed toward the

staircase, Olive realized she had seconds to make her move before the hallway became a trap with no escape routes.

The kitchen and back door were her only chance.

But getting there meant timing her movements perfectly and hoping that fifteen years of training would be enough to get her out of this house alive.

Max's heavy footsteps entered the hallway, and Olive knew she was out of time and options.

With no other choice, she abandoned stealth entirely and ran.

She sprinted toward the back of the house, her shoes slapping against the hardwood as shouts erupted behind her.

The kitchen doorway seemed impossibly far away, and she heard both men moving now—Max's thundering pursuit and the silver-haired man barking orders into what was probably a radio.

"Stop! Security breach!"

Olive hit the back door at full speed, grateful it was still unlocked from her entry. She burst outside into the late afternoon air and immediately veered toward the tree line, hoping the forest would provide cover for her escape route back to the festival grounds.

Behind her, the door slammed open as Max chased her outside.

"There! Heading for the woods!"

She had to move—and fast.

Because she was certain if she was caught, she'd mysteriously disappear also.

CHAPTER 47

Olive rushed through the underbrush, branches tearing at her clothes and scratching her exposed skin.

Her cap was knocked off by a low-hanging branch within the first fifty yards.

A few seconds later, her sweatshirt caught on a thorn bush.

She abandoned it rather than wasting precious seconds trying to free herself.

The sound of pursuit was getting closer.

Max crashed through the forest behind her with the subtlety of a bulldozer, and at least one other person had joined the chase. They shouted coordinates to each other, trying to predict her route and cut her off.

Olive had some distinct advantages: She was

lighter and faster than her pursuers, and she'd memorized the terrain during her approach to the house. She knew exactly where she was going.

The festival sounds grew louder ahead of her—music, voices, the general noise of a crowd gathered for a performance. Safety was within reach, but she had to get there before these men caught up to her in the woods where no one would witness what happened next.

Twenty more feet through the trees and she'd be at the edge of the crowd.

Fifteen feet.

Ten.

Five feet.

She burst from the trees and immediately forced herself to slow down. She had to transition from a desperate sprint to what looked like a casual jog as she approached the back of the crowd gathered around the makeshift stage.

One misstep could seal her fate.

Olive pushed herself through the outer edge of the festival attendees, trying to control her breathing and appear like someone who'd simply been taking a nature walk rather than fleeing for her life.

Her heart hammered against her ribs and sweat

beaded on her forehead despite the cool mountain air.

She spotted Jason near the center of the crowd, standing with Tristan and a few other festivalgoers as they watched what appeared to be another terrible performance by local musicians.

Moving carefully through the assembled people, she made her way toward him, forcing her expression into something that looked bored rather than terrified.

"There you are," Jason said when she appeared beside him, his voice casual but his eyes sharp with concern. "I was starting to wonder where you'd wandered off to."

"Just needed some air." Olive hoped her voice sounded steadier than she felt. "This music is . . ."

"Painful," Tristan finished for her. "I've heard better performances in London subway stations."

But even as she tried to engage in normal conversation, Olive's attention was focused on the trees behind them.

At any minute, her pursuers would catch up.

When they did, would they identify her? She prayed that wouldn't be the case.

CHAPTER 48

Within moments, two figures emerged from the forest—Max and Tom.

They stood at the edge of the crowd, their eyes scanning the festivalgoers with the methodical precision of hunters searching for prey. Max's face was flushed from the chase, his expensive hiking boots now scuffed and dirty from crashing through the underbrush.

Olive kept her head down, using Jason's taller frame to partially shield her from view while she watched the security team's search pattern.

They were looking for someone who matched her general description—a woman in dark clothing who'd been inside the house, where she definitely didn't belong.

Without her cap and hoodie, and now wearing

just a plain gray T-shirt and jeans, Olive looked like dozens of other female festival attendees.

But if they got close enough . . .

Max's gaze swept across the crowd, moving from person to person. When his attention passed over their general area, Olive turned slightly toward Jason as if he'd said something interesting.

She held her breath as Max's scan continued, his frustration evident in his body language. Tom worked the other side of the crowd, but neither of them seemed to be having any luck identifying their target among the sea of festivalgoers.

After what felt like an eternity, Max pulled out his radio and spoke into it. Olive couldn't hear the words over the terrible music from the stage.

Then both men turned and headed back toward the trees, apparently giving up their search for the moment.

Olive waited until they'd completely disappeared into the forest before allowing herself to back away from Jason and breathe normally again.

"Everything okay?" Jason asked. "What happened?"

"The important thing is that I got what we came for. We need to talk. Soon."

She'd just escaped by the skin of her teeth.

But the information she'd gathered about the Grayfall experiment was worth the risk.

Now they had to figure out how to use it to save Chloe, Becca, and everyone else before Phase 3 of whatever nightmare they'd stumbled into began in earnest.

Jason guided Olive away from the crowd, leading her to the old mercantile building, which would provide shelter from prying eyes. The old stone walls offered both physical cover and psychological distance from the security team that had been hunting her.

Stepping through the partially collapsed doorway, they entered what had once been Grayfall's commercial heart. The interior was a ghost of its former self—empty wooden shelves lined the walls like skeletal ribs, their surfaces warped and splintered from decades of weather exposure. Behind what had been the main counter, cubbyholes and small drawers hung open, their contents long since claimed by time and scavengers.

The floorboards sagged dangerously in places where the foundation had shifted, creating treacherous dips and valleys that required careful navigation. Scattered across the uneven surface were the remnants of the store's final days: rusted cans with illegible labels, fragments of glass from broken jars, and scraps of fabric that might once have been work clothes or household textiles.

Overhead, gaps in the roof allowed shafts of late afternoon sunlight to filter through, illuminating dust motes that danced in the still air. The space smelled of old wood, rust, and something vaguely sweet—perhaps the lingering scent of bulk goods that had rotted away long ago.

Despite the decay, the building's thick stone walls provided excellent acoustics for private conversation, muffling outside sounds while amplifying whispers between them. It was exactly the kind of sanctuary they needed to process what Olive had discovered in Brad's house without fear of being overheard.

"Are you okay?" Jason's voice sounded tight with worry as he turned to face her, his hands automatically moving to check for injuries. "You were gone so long, and then I saw those men searching the crowd . . ."

"I'm fine," Olive said, though her hands were still shaking from the adrenaline crash. "But, Jason, what I found in that house—"

Before she could continue, he pulled her into his arms, holding her tightly against his chest. The embrace was fierce, desperate, carrying all the fear and relief he'd been holding back while watching her nearly get caught.

"I should have never let you go there alone," he

murmured into her hair. "When I saw them come out of the woods looking for someone . . ."

"I know." Olive allowed herself a moment to absorb his warmth and strength.

Despite everything between them, despite all the reasons she'd been keeping her distance, being in Jason's arms felt like coming home.

But they couldn't afford to lose focus now—not since she'd found out the information they needed.

CHAPTER 49

Olive pulled back slightly, though she remained within the circle of Jason's arms. "Jason, this isn't a festival scam. It's so much worse than that."

She quickly told him about what she'd found—the lists of employees, the projections, the financials. She told him about the conversation she'd overheard Elias having about people dying.

"I have a feeling this was never about the festival," she explained. "This festival was an excuse, a way of covering up equipment and people coming in and out of this area. It's ruse meant to disguise something much bigger. I'm just not sure what."

Jason's expression grew darker with each detail. "And not everyone is supposed to survive."

"Exactly. Chloe and Becca must have gotten too

nosy, too close to the truth." Olive glanced around nervously, making sure they weren't being overheard. "We need to talk to Tevin. Maybe he can find out more about who's really running this operation. Because this is bigger than Brad. He's the face behind it but not the brains."

"Agreed," Jason said, though his protective instincts clearly warred with the practical need to continue their investigation. "But we also need to be more careful. If they realize you were in that house . . ."

"I know." Olive's throat tightened as she scanned the area again. There were no clear signs of surveillance. "The question is, how many other secrets are hiding in this place? And how many of these people aren't who they seem to be?"

Olive and Jason made their way back toward the main stage area where the opening act was finishing their set to scattered, unenthusiastic applause.

The crowd looked both exhausted and demoralized, their initial excitement for the weekend completely drained by the poor conditions and constant disappointments.

Olive would have loved to be anywhere but here, listening to awful music among increasingly unhappy festivalgoers. The rational part of her mind wondered why people weren't demanding to leave en masse.

That question was answered when Brad climbed back onto the stage, his smile looking more strained than ever.

"I know today has been challenging," he announced. "But I have incredible news that's going to make everything worth it!"

Somehow, Olive doubted that.

A large screen descended behind him, displaying the logo for Obscurity—the headliner many people had actually paid to see.

"Due to transportation difficulties, Obscurity couldn't make it here in person today," Brad continued over the crowd's disappointed groans. "But they've recorded a special message just for you!"

The screen lit up with a video message from the band, promising they would definitely perform tomorrow night if people could just "hang in there" a little longer. The lead singer looked directly into the camera as he said, "Grayfall Festival is going to be legendary. Don't give up on us now—we're going to make this worth every penny you paid."

Olive watched as hope flickered back to life in some faces around her. These people had paid enormous amounts of money specifically to see Obscurity, and the promise of tomorrow night's performance was apparently enough to keep them from leaving.

"Brilliant crowd control," Jason murmured. "Keep dangling the carrot just out of reach."

As the video ended and Brad introduced the next local act, Olive's blood turned to ice.

Walking onto the stage with a guitar was the pale-eyed man from Murphy's Last Stop gas station.

CHAPTER 50

He was the same man who'd tried to assault Olive, the one she'd humiliated in front of his friend.

He looked different cleaned up and holding his guitar, but there was no mistaking those cold, predatory eyes.

And as the band began their first song, his eyes found her in the crowd.

Recognition flashed across the man's face, followed immediately by something dark and vengeful. His fingers never stopped moving on the guitar strings, and his voice never wavered as he sang.

But his gaze remained locked on Olive with unmistakable malice.

Jason tensed beside her as he noticed the dangerous attention. "Olive . . ."

"We need to move," she whispered. "Now."

But as they began to ease back through the crowd, Pale Eyes leaned closer to his microphone and spoke directly to the audience.

"This next song goes out to a special lady in the crowd." His voice carried clearly over the sound system. "Someone who taught me that what goes around, comes around."

As people began glancing around, Olive's muscles tensed.

"Do you have any idea what he's talking about?" Jason whispered.

"Unfortunately, I do."

Her problems had just multiplied exponentially. Not only was she being hunted by Brad's security team, but now she had a personal enemy with access to a microphone and a crowd of witnesses.

The question was whether she could disappear into the audience before he found a way to point her out to everyone—including the people who were already looking for her.

When the band took their break between sets, Olive disappeared into the crowd. It seemed like the best place to hide.

But Pale Eyes must have been watching.

He appeared beside her as if materializing from the shadows, moving with the predatory confidence of someone who felt he had the upper hand.

Up close, he looked more dangerous than he had at the gas station. The veneer of being halfway civilized made his underlying menace more pronounced rather than less.

"Well, well." His voice, practically a growl, was low enough that only she and Jason could hear it over the noise of the crowd. "Look who we got here. Thought you could embarrass me and just walk away?"

"I don't know what you're talking about." Olive kept her voice calm, though every muscle in her body tensed for action.

"Right, you don't." Pale Eyes stepped closer, invading her personal space in a way that was clearly meant to intimidate. "You cost me face in front of my friend. Made me look like a fool."

Jason moved slightly, positioning himself between Olive and the aggressive musician.

"I think there's been some misunderstanding," he said diplomatically. "Maybe we should just—"

"Ain't talking to you, pretty boy," Pale Eyes snarled, trying to push past Jason to get closer to Olive. "This is between me and the little wildcat here."

"No, it's not." Jason's voice carried a warning that

made several nearby festivalgoers look over curiously.

Pale Eyes didn't appear to recognize the danger signals. He grabbed Olive's arm, his fingers digging into her skin. "You're gonna learn some respect—"

"You have two seconds to let go of her arm," Jason growled.

Pale Eyes ignored him. "I was dreamin' about running into you here—"

Before he could say anything else, Jason's fist connected with the man's jaw.

CHAPTER 51

The impact sent Pale Eyes staggering backward, releasing Olive's arm as he fought to keep his balance.

But instead of backing down, Pale Eyes came back swinging.

What followed was less a fight than a brawl, with both men grappling and throwing punches while festivalgoers scattered to give them room. Jason had training and technique on his side, but Pale Eyes fought dirty, going for eye gouges and kidney shots that forced Jason to adapt his approach.

Within seconds, other people got involved—some trying to break up the fight, others taking sides based on nothing more than crowd dynamics. Shouts erupted from multiple directions as the situation spiraled out of control.

"Fight! Fight!"

"Someone stop them!"

"Where's security?"

The chaos lasted less than two minutes before Max appeared, cutting through the crowd with authority.

He stood between the men, arms outstretched, and separated them. "Enough!"

Olive had hoped not to draw any unnecessary attention.

That clearly hadn't happened.

In fact, now everyone was watching them.

Max led both men behind the old buildings in town, away from the crowd and the continuing chaos their fight had created.

Olive followed. Leaving Jason alone with Max wasn't an option given what she'd overheard in Brad's house.

Max turned toward both men, standing between them like a referee maintaining separation.

"What was that about?" Max demanded, his attention focused primarily on Jason. "You can't just start throwing punches because someone talks to your wife."

"He grabbed her." Jason glowered at Pale Eyes. "Hard enough to leave marks."

"Bull," Pale Eyes spat, though his jaw was already swelling from Jason's initial punch. "I was just having a conversation with the lady."

"A conversation that involved putting your hands on me without permission." Olive rolled up her sleeve to show the finger-shaped bruises already forming on her arm.

Max's expression darkened as he saw the marks, and for a moment Olive thought she detected genuine disgust in his face.

Then his professional mask slipped back into place. "Okay, everyone needs to cool down. Bobby, get back to the stage. Your band's got another set to play."

"This ain't over," Pale Eyes—apparently named Bobby—muttered as he headed back toward the festival area. He shot one last venomous look at Olive. "Not by a long shot."

CHAPTER 52

After Pale Eyes/Bobby left, Max turned his attention to Jason and Olive. "You want to tell me what really happened here? Because that seemed personal."

Olive made a quick decision. If Max was having doubts about the operation—and her overheard conversation suggested he was—maybe she could use that to her advantage.

"I ran into him at a gas station on my way here," she said. "He tried to assault me when I asked for directions. My husband wasn't there, so I had to defend myself."

He narrowed his eyes. "Defend yourself how?"

"I have some self-defense training. Nothing fancy, but enough to get away from someone who doesn't understand what 'no' means."

Max studied her face as if trying to assess the truth of her statement. His expression was unreadable, but she sensed something shifting in his attitude.

"These mountains can be dangerous for outsiders," he finally said. "Local law enforcement doesn't always . . . respond quickly to certain types of incidents."

There was something in his tone—a weariness, a hint of disgust—that made Olive think he'd seen this kind of situation before. And that he hadn't liked it.

"Max, you seem like someone who actually cares about people's safety." Olive paused. "Can I ask you something?"

His guard immediately went up. "Depends on the question."

"Are you happy with how this festival is being run? Because from where I'm sitting, it looks like people are being unnecessarily put in danger."

For just a moment, Max's professional facade cracked. She saw frustration, moral conflict, and what might have been regret flash across his features.

Would he share?

Olive held her breath as she waited, praying this worked and that she could turn him.

Max opened his mouth as if he was going to share something.

Then he clamped his lips together, and his gaze hardened. "I don't discuss operational details with guests."

"If you know about something that's going on here—"

"I was just hired to do a job," Max said. "Nothing more, nothing less."

"So you're going to sit back and do nothing while other people get hurt?" Olive stared at him. "I can see it in your eyes. That bothers you."

He stared straight ahead and grunted.

Olive sensed he was struggling with what to do.

She waited, hoping her words had gotten through to him. Jason remained quiet, probably realizing Olive had a better chance of getting through to Max—especially after what had just happened.

He could be their chance to find out more information.

Finally, he looked back at Olive, resolve hardening in his gaze. "You and your husband should focus on enjoying the rest of your weekend and staying out of trouble."

Her shoulders sagged with disappointment.

They'd been so close. But something had him spooked enough to stay quiet.

Was someone threatening him also?

The warning in his voice was clear: He wouldn't answer questions, but he also wouldn't necessarily act against them if they stayed under the radar.

It wasn't the alliance Olive had hoped for, but it wasn't outright hostility either. Since her enemies seemed to outnumber her potential allies, even neutral parties might prove valuable.

The question was whether Max's apparent moral conflicts would eventually override his professional obligations—and whether that would happen in time to make a difference.

CHAPTER 53

Max grumbled that Olive and Jason needed to stay put for a while.

He arranged for dinner to be brought to them as they sat behind the old pharmacy. The meal arrived courtesy of the same overwhelmed catering staff, and it was every bit as disappointing as everything else about the festival experience.

Two paper bowls containing what appeared to be canned chili, plus a bag full of stale crackers and warm sodas—hardly the "gourmet wilderness dining experience" that had been advertised.

Olive and Jason sat side by side at an old picnic table. She picked at the congealed mess, while Jason ate mechanically, his attention clearly focused on something other than the disgusting food.

The silence between them stretched uncomfortably until he finally set down his plastic spoon and looked directly at her.

"Why didn't you tell me about what happened at the gas station?" His voice was quiet but carried an undertone of hurt. "I asked you if you had any problems getting here, and you said everything was fine."

Olive's stomach clenched—and it wasn't because of the questionable chili. "I didn't think it was relevant to our investigation."

"A man tried to assault you, and you had to physically defend yourself. How is that not relevant?" Jason's tone grew more intense. "What if he'd had a weapon? What if there had been more of them? What if—"

"I handled it," Olive interrupted. "I've been handling things like that for years."

"That's not the point." Jason pushed his plate away, his food barely touched. "The point is that we're supposed to be partners, and partners don't keep secrets that could affect their safety or the mission."

The irony of his words hit Olive like a physical blow.

Here he was, lecturing her about keeping secrets when she'd been wrestling with the biggest secret of all—the connection between his father's business and her family's house, the questions about whether

Jason himself might somehow be connected to her parents' murder.

"Or is it because you don't trust me?" Jason continued, his voice growing quieter but more pointed. "Because that's what this feels like, Olive. Like you still don't trust me enough to be honest about what's happening."

Olive stared at her untouched dinner, her mind racing. How did she respond?

The hurt in Jason's voice was genuine, and Olive knew he had every right to feel betrayed by her omission.

But how could she explain that trust wasn't the issue—that it was love that made her keep secrets? That she was so terrified of losing him again that she'd rather suffer in silence than risk discovering he was connected to the worst tragedy of her life?

"What aren't you telling me?" Jason asked, his voice soft. "Because I know there's something. I've known since the day I started at Aegis. You've been keeping me at arm's length, and I can't figure out why."

Olive's hands trembled slightly as she gripped her soda can. This was the moment—the conversation she'd been dreading and avoiding in equal measure.

She could tell him about the house, about the investigation into his father's business dealings, about her suspicions and fears. She could finally be honest about why she'd been so careful to maintain professional distance between them.

But sitting behind an abandoned building in the middle of a music festival scam run by people willing to silence anyone who was a threat, surrounded by enemies and uncertain allies, seemed like the worst possible time to have a conversation that might destroy whatever trust they'd managed to rebuild.

"Jason . . ." she began, then stopped, unsure how to continue.

"It's about my father, isn't it?" Jason's voice was resigned rather than angry. "Something you found during your background investigation of me."

Olive's breath caught. "How did you—"

"Because I know you, Olive. And I know you'd never trust anyone blindly, especially not someone from your past who suddenly reappeared in your life." Jason's smile was sad rather than bitter. "I figured you'd run a full background check on me and everyone in my family. The question is what you found that made you decide I might be dangerous."

CHAPTER 54

Before Olive could formulate a response, Tevin slipped behind the building, heading toward them. His expression was grim as he assessed their faces.

"Sorry to interrupt." His tone, however, suggested he wasn't entirely sorry to break up what looked like an intense conversation. "But I needed to check in with you both. The security situation is escalating."

A mixture of relief and frustration twisted inside Olive at the interruption. The conversation with Jason would have to wait—again.

"What kind of escalation?" Jason shifted into professional mode despite the personal tension still hanging between them.

"More search teams are being deployed. They're

looking for someone who was in an unauthorized area this afternoon." Tevin's gaze moved to Olive. "Someone who might have accessed sensitive information."

Olive's heart thumped harder. Her. They were looking for her.

Her only hope was that no one could identify her. She'd kept her eyes open for security cameras, but she hadn't seen any.

"How much trouble are we in?" Olive asked.

Tevin leveled his gaze with her. "Depends on what you found and whether they can prove you were there."

Olive briefed Tevin on her discoveries in Brad's house.

Tevin's expression grew darker with each detail. "This is so much worse than we thought."

"Can you find out more about who's funding this?" Olive asked. "The government connections?"

"I'll see what I can dig up, but it's going to take time. And given the security situation . . ." Tevin shook his head. "What's our next move?"

"I want to find out what those tents were there for," Olive said. "I can't help but feel like they might provide some answers. Then I want to see inside the mine. We need evidence of whatever is happening there."

"Going into the mine is not just dangerous, it's suicide," Tevin rushed. "We don't know the layout, the security measures, or what's going on down there."

"It's a bad idea," Jason agreed, though Olive saw the conflict in his gaze. "There has to be another way."

"What other way?" Olive's voice carried her frustration.

Tevin let out a sigh. "First, check out those tents. I'll set up a distraction so you can get away."

"A distraction?" Jason asked.

Tevin frowned but nodded. "I'll get Maya to help. She's really good at doing things to draw attention."

Olive tilted her head, sensing there was more to his words. "What do you mean?"

"I caught her today. She was in the middle of hiding some speakers around town—speakers that would play ghostly sounds. She confessed to me that she's set up a few things."

"Like what?" Jason asked even though they all probably knew the answer.

"She planted that dead bird on her car, for starters. And she left that blood—which wasn't really blood, of course, on the rocks on the hiking trail when no one was looking. And, of course, she made up the story about her tent being ransacked and the glowing red eyes. She's doing it all for views. The more drama, the more people watch her videos and the more income she gets."

Olive shook her head at the audacity—and desperation—of some people. "I should have known."

"Are any of us really surprised?" Tevin raised his brow.

"No, we're not." Olive paused. "Are you sure you want to cause a distraction? It's going to bring attention to you, and I don't know if that's a good idea."

"I can handle this. Believe me. Just give me fifteen minutes. When I do that, you guys can go and check out those tents. The festival is over tomorrow so we don't have much more time."

Before Tevin walked away, she grabbed his arm. He looked back at her, his pupils growing larger.

"Be careful," she murmured. "Please."

He stared at her another moment before withdrawing his arm. "I will be. You too. I'm not leaving this assignment by myself. The three of us came in together, and the three of us are leaving together."

Olive nodded as she heard the worry in his voice. "It's a deal."

CHAPTER 55

True to his word, Tevin's distraction came exactly fifteen minutes later in the form of a heated argument with one of the catering staff about food safety violations.

His voice carried clearly across the festival grounds as he demanded to speak to management about the "health department violations" he'd allegedly witnessed. Maya piped in also, her phone raised and camera rolling as she caught all the drama. Tevin even threw in something about the Dark Watchers being involved, how they wanted to harm people at the festival.

Good job, Tevin.

As security personnel and curious festivalgoers gravitated toward the drama, Olive and Jason slipped away from the crowd and into the trees behind the old mercantile building.

The forest was thicker than it had appeared from a distance, with overlapping canopies that blocked most of the remaining daylight. They moved carefully through the underbrush, using game trails when possible to minimize noise and avoid leaving obvious tracks.

They carefully passed by Brad's house and continued deeper into the forest.

She paused at one point, realizing there were narrow backroads cutting through the forest. She shouldn't be surprised.

But, for some reason, organizers had wanted festivalgoers to hike to the site. Why was that?

She and Jason hiked in silence, their earlier conversation still unresolved. But this wasn't the time to dive into that. That talk demanded their full attention.

"There," Jason whispered after they'd been walking for about ten minutes.

Through a gap in the trees ahead, Olive saw the temporary camp she'd spotted from Brad's place. But as they crept closer to get a better view, her stomach clenched with a mixture of anger and understanding.

The encampment was larger than she'd expected. There were at least two dozen tents arranged in rough rows, with a central area containing what appeared to be cooking facilities and basic sanitation. Two other large buildings had been erected on the other side. Each structure had been painted an olive-green color, almost as if to camouflage them.

Clothes hung from makeshift lines strung between trees, and she could hear the quiet murmur of conversations in Spanish drifting through the evening air.

"Migrant workers," Jason said.

"Living in conditions even worse than the festival accommodations." Olive felt sick as she took in the scene.

People here were clearly making do with minimal resources. They'd been hidden away where no one would see them or ask questions about their presence.

The question was: Why? What were these people being forced to do in hiding?

As Olive and Jason watched from their concealed position, she noticed details that painted a troubling picture.

The workers moved with the careful efficiency of people who'd been living this way for weeks or months. Children played quietly between the tents while adults prepared simple meals over small camp stoves.

"Hector," Jason said suddenly.

Olive knew he was thinking the same thing she was.

The missing worker who'd supposedly just "left" without collecting his pay. Had he really left, or had he discovered something that made him a liability?

She knew what her guess was.

"This is bigger than we thought," Olive whispered. "Way bigger."

They weren't just dealing with a fraudulent festival or even simple criminal activity. This was an operation that required a substantial workforce, people who could be kept hidden and controlled, people whose disappearance wouldn't necessarily be investigated by authorities.

The implications were staggering.

"The mine." Jason's tone sounded grim with determination. "Now more than ever we have to check out the mine."

Olive nodded, watching as the last light faded from the sky above them. The timing couldn't be better. Full darkness would provide cover for their approach.

Questions tumbled in her mind, the biggest being whether she and Jason were prepared for what they might find when they finally made it inside that mountain.

CHAPTER 56

Olive wished there was a way she and Jason could get to the other two buildings near the campsites, but it was too risky. There was no way to get inside without being caught.

She turned to Jason as they threaded their way through the woods. "Do you think Brad is trying to extract any leftover coal or something?"

He shook his head, his jaw tightening. "No, it would be noisier. There would be more equipment."

"So what exactly is going on? What is so important that these people are willing to either abduct people or worse in order to not ruin their plan?"

"That's a good question. But I echo Tevin's concerns about going in the mine. It's risky. Once we're in there, we're essentially trapped."

"I think we need to take that risk."

His jaw flexed again. "I don't like the idea of you being in there."

She appreciated his concern. She really did.

But she had a job to do, and his feelings for her couldn't get in the way.

She placed a hand on his forearm. "Jason, if you weren't with me this wouldn't even be a consideration. It's just part of doing my job."

Something washed through his gaze. The reality of working together was settling on him. He would see her in risky situations. It came with the territory.

His gaze hardened before he finally said, "We, at least, need to call Rex and let him know what's going on. Just in case something happens and all three of us are taken out."

Olive nodded. "We'll probably have reception once we get closer to Brad's house. We'll let him know. If he doesn't hear back from us, he should send in backup."

Jason's neck looked stiff as he nodded. "Let's do that. But for the record, I don't like this."

Olive and Jason bypassed going back to the festival site.

Instead, after talking with Rex, they went right to the mine. There was no time to waste.

The lock on the gate of the chain link fence at the mine's entrance was old and corroded.

Olive's lock-picking skills made quick work of it.

She and Jason slipped through the opening and moved into the shadows cast by the twisted metal support beams that framed the mine entrance. The contrast between the festival's chaotic energy and the oppressive silence of this place was jarring—as if they'd stepped from one world into another entirely.

"Stay close." Jason pulled out a small flashlight and shielded its beam with his fingers to minimize the visible light.

Rusty railroad tracks disappeared into the darkness ahead—twin lines of corroded steel that had once carried coal cars but now served as a path deeper into the mountain's belly.

Water dripped steadily from somewhere in the darkness above. Each drop echoed with a hollow ping as it hit the metal rails or pooled in the spaces between rotting railroad ties. The wooden crossbeams that supported the tunnel showed signs of age and neglect—some sagged dangerously, while others had splintered entirely, leaving jagged fragments hanging like broken teeth.

Along the walls, old mining equipment sat abandoned where it had been left decades ago: rusted pickaxes, overturned coal cars, and lengths of cable that looked like dead snakes in the shifting beam of the flashlight.

But it was the smell that made the space feel most oppressive—not just the expected odors of abandonment, but something that suggested the mountain itself was slowly reclaiming this artificial wound, filling it with moisture and decay until nothing remained of human ambition but rust and shadows.

They'd advanced maybe twenty feet into the tunnel when Jason's flashlight beam caught something that made them both freeze.

A body lay crumpled against the tunnel wall, partially hidden behind a rusted piece of mining equipment.

Even in the dim light, Olive recognized the weathered features and mountain clothing.

Her pulse raced.

It was the Grayfall Guardian.

CHAPTER 57

"No . . ." Olive gasped, temporarily stunned.

Jason quickly scanned the area for immediate threats before moving closer to examine the body. The Guardian had been shot twice in the chest, the dark stains on his flannel shirt still wet enough to gleam in the flashlight's beam.

"This just happened," Jason said. "Maybe within the last hour."

Olive's stomach clenched with guilt and anger. The man had tried to warn them, had risked his own safety to give cryptic but genuine alerts about the danger they were walking into.

Now he was dead because someone had decided he knew too much.

"He was trying to help us." Olive's voice was

thick with emotion. "All those warnings. He knew what was happening here."

Jason examined the Guardian's hands, and his expression suddenly changed. "Olive, look at this."

The man's right hand clutched something—a piece of paper that had been folded and refolded multiple times until it was barely larger than a business card. Olive carefully extracted it from the man's grip, careful not to disturb any evidence.

As she unfolded the paper, Jason moved closer, standing partially behind her and looking over her shoulder.

The paper contained a hand-drawn map, sketched in pencil. It showed the mine's tunnel system.

But it was the words written at the bottom of the map that made Olive's blood run cold.

"SAVE THEM" was scrawled in dark letters that looked like they'd been written with the Guardian's own blood, probably in his final moments before death claimed him.

Olive and Jason studied the map's details. The chambers were all spelled out.

"He knew something was going on down here," Olive murmured.

"He died to get this information," Jason added.

"We can't let his sacrifice be meaningless. We have to keep going." Her voice shook as she said the words.

Jason looked at her with an expression that mixed admiration and concern. "We're walking into an active crime scene with people who are willing to eliminate anyone who threatens their operation."

"I know. But Chloe and Becca and whoever else they might be holding don't have time for us to be cautious. If we wait for backup or try to work through official channels, more people are going to end up like him." Olive gestured toward the Guardian's still form.

Both of them seemed to feel the weight of what they saw. An innocent man, killed for trying to do the right thing. A team was probably on the way, ready to clean up the mess of his death.

That meant they didn't have much time.

It wouldn't surprise her if there was a string of dead bodies traced back to this location.

But why? That was the question echoing in her mind.

Why was someone doing all this? What made someone think human lives were expendable?

CHAPTER 58

Following the Guardian's hand-drawn map, Olive and Jason continued farther into the dark mine.

A few minutes later, they descended what appeared to be a newer staircase carved directly into the mountain rock.

At the bottom, they emerged into what felt like another world.

Harsh white LED arrays turned the tunnel system into what resembled a high-tech manufacturing facility rather than an abandoned mine. The tunnels had given way to some type of industrial operation. Ventilation systems pumped fresh air into the passages.

In the distance, they saw workers—probably

twenty—bent over conveyor belts while guards monitored the perimeter.

Olive and Jason stayed in the shadows, careful not to be seen.

"What in the world?" Jason whispered, staring at the scene before them.

"This isn't some small-scale illegal dig," Olive murmured, snapping a couple of pictures. "This is a full industrial extraction facility."

"I've never seen anything like it."

Neither had Olive. But the sophisticated equipment was being used to extract . . . something.

Whatever it was, it wasn't coal.

This was more than Olive had ever envisioned.

The stakes were higher.

And that made this situation much worse.

The sound of approaching footsteps echoed from somewhere deep in the facility—multiple sets of boots, moving with purpose toward their location.

"We need to go," Jason whispered. "Now."

They'd seen enough to understand the scope of what they were dealing with. The evidence on Olive's phone could bring down the entire plan.

But only if they lived long enough to share it.

The footsteps came closer, accompanied by voices

discussing shift changes and security protocols. Olive and Jason ducked behind a thick metal cart that had probably been left behind from coal-mining days.

"The next extraction cycle starts at 0200," someone said. "And the surface operations should be completed before dawn."

"Perfect," another voice said. "Make sure the perimeter stays secure."

The voices faded as the workers continued deeper into the facility.

Olive knew she and Jason couldn't risk staying any longer. They'd pushed their luck far enough already.

They made their way back through the tunnel system, moving as quickly as they dared. The Guardian's body still lay there. A crew hadn't been back yet to clean up the crime.

But they'd be here soon—Olive was certain of it.

When she and Jason finally emerged from the mine entrance, the cool night air felt like freedom itself.

They hadn't been caught.

Now they just had to keep it that way . . . unless they wanted to end up like the Guardian.

CHAPTER 59

Back in Grayfall, Olive noted that most people had apparently given up on the evening's entertainment and retreated to their tents. Despite that, another terrible band performed in the distance—probably more "local talent" Brad had promised would make up for the missing headliners.

"We need to look at those photos you took earlier," Jason said as they approached their tent. "Maybe they have the answers we need."

Olive nodded, her adrenaline slowly fading as the magnitude of their discovery settled over her. They huddled inside their cramped tent and scrolled through the images she'd captured.

"Wait." Jason pointed to one of the photos. "Go back to that last one."

Olive found the image he was referring to—a

schedule she'd photographed that detailed various operational phases and timing. As she studied it more carefully, a pattern emerged.

"Look at this." She enlarged the text. "Six a.m. to eight a.m.—Surface Operations Minimal, Shift Change Window. And here—Security Patrols Reduced During Equipment Maintenance."

Jason studied the schedule more carefully. "Those auxiliary facilities—they have to be those buildings near the migrant camp we spotted. If they're doing weekly inspections, that means the buildings will be temporarily unoccupied."

"It's risky." Even as Olive said the words, she could already see the possibility forming. "But it might be our only chance to find out what's really happening to people like Hector."

The missing worker's fate had taken on new significance now that they'd seen the scope of the operation. If he'd discovered what they'd just discovered, his disappearance might not have been voluntary at all.

"Six a.m.," Jason agreed. "We'll need to move fast and be ready to get out quickly if things go wrong."

As they sat in their compact tent, the photos from the mine still glowing on Olive's phone screen, the pieces of the puzzle finally clicked into place with devastating clarity.

"The festival was never real," she said quietly,

scrolling through her photos. "It was just an elaborate cover."

Jason looked up from studying the schedule they'd found. "What do you mean?"

"Think about it." Olive's voice grew more urgent as the connections formed in her mind. "All the heavy equipment Brad claimed was for 'stage construction'—it was really mining machinery being moved into position. The helicopters supposedly bringing in musicians were actually transporting industrial supplies."

"They needed an excuse for all the activity, all the noise, all the people coming and going," Jason finished.

Nausea roiled inside Olive as she understood the scope of the deception. "What do you think they're extracting?"

"I'm thinking maybe there are rare earth minerals that were found in those mine shafts. They're using migrant workers, hiding the operation underground, and eliminating anyone who gets too close to the truth."

Horrible music still drifted across the campsite from the main stage, and now even that took on sinister implications. Local musicians keeping people distracted while the real work happened underground and in the hidden facilities.

"But why Chloe and Becca?" Jason asked. "If this

is just about illegal mining, why target them specifically?"

Olive stared at the photos, her mind racing. "Because they saw too much. Chloe was supposed to create promotional content that made this place look authentic, but she must have learned something she wasn't supposed to know. And Becca . . ."

"Her friend must have overheard something when she interned for Brad," Jason finished. "Becca came here to investigate, and someone got suspicious . . ."

The stakes were too high right now for them to mess up, Olive pondered as pressure built between her shoulders.

This was one assignment she couldn't fail.

"This goes way beyond Brad Kellerman. He can't be running this." Certainty grew in Olive's voice. "He's just the front man. This kind of operation requires massive funding, government connections, sophisticated equipment."

Jason nodded. "Someone with serious resources is backing this. Someone who can make people disappear and make mining operations look like music festivals."

"We need to let Rex and Tevin know."

"I'll call Rex with the update." Jason rose. "You've already risked enough."

"But—"

"No buts. I'll walk close to Brad's house and make the call. I'll be careful. I'll stop by Tevin's tent on the way back."

Olive knew better than to argue. Instead, she nodded.

But the gravity of this situation pressed on her. The people behind this had too much money involved for them to back down without a fight.

And there would be a fight.

But how many people would become collateral damage in the process?

Outside their tent, the music continued—a soundtrack to one of the most elaborate criminal conspiracies Olive had ever encountered.

And somewhere in the darkness, two young women were depending on Olive and Jason to uncover the truth before it was too late—if it wasn't already.

CHAPTER 60

ELEVEN YEARS AGO, BLUE RIDGE MOUNTAINS, GEORGIA

That night, as Olive's family and the Hendersons shared a dinner of grilled chicken and potatoes around the campfire, Dad pulled out his leather journal and began sketching detailed maps of their discoveries, documenting every find.

They'd managed to locate several other treasures on their hike before going back to their campsite.

The Hendersons continued to hang on his every word as he explained the historical significance of each artifact, the careful research that had led them to these locations, and the potential value of the main treasure they were still seeking.

"James," Mr. Henderson started. "I have to ask—would you ever consider taking on investment partners for future expeditions? This seems like exactly the kind of unique opportunity my portfolio has been missing."

Dad looked surprised, as if the idea had never occurred to him. "Well, I . . . I suppose if I found the right partners, people who really understood the historical significance of this work . . ."

"We're talking about serious money here, aren't we?" Mrs. Henderson added. "If these preliminary finds are any indication . . ."

"Conservative estimates suggest we're looking at mid-six figures for the main cache," Dad said. "But, of course, treasure hunting always involves risk. I'd never want to take someone's investment unless they were completely comfortable with the uncertainties involved."

Olive watched the conversation unfold with growing unease. The Hendersons were intelligent, successful people. But they were also caught up in the excitement of discovery, the romance of hidden treasure, and the compelling narrative her father had constructed around Cornelius Slattery's fictional fortune.

When the adults moved away from the fire to discuss "business details," Olive found herself staring at the collection of artifacts spread across Dad's journal—the compass, old coins, pieces of jewelry that told a story of Confederate gold hidden in Georgia mountains.

In the firelight, everything looked authentic, valuable, historically significant. Just like Dad's explanations always sounded reasonable until she thought about them too carefully.

Several minutes later, as the adults chatted, the kids went to their tents to turn in for the evening.

"Ollie?" Jessie whispered from her sleeping bag. "Are we really going to be rich?"

"I don't know," Olive whispered back, listening to the low murmur of adult voices discussing investment amounts and partnership agreements. "I honestly don't know."

But she was beginning to suspect that the only treasure her father was really hunting was the contents of the Henderson family's bank account.

CHAPTER 61

PRESENT DAY

Olive's phone alarm vibrated silently against her wrist at 5:30 a.m., pulling her from the uneasy sleep she'd finally managed in the hour before dawn.

The festival grounds were completely quiet now. The terrible music had stopped hours ago, leaving only the sound of the river rushing past the campsite.

Jason was already awake beside her, his eyes open as he stared at the tent ceiling. She suspected his mind raced with what they might find today.

She prayed it would be Chloe and Becca alive.

"Ready?" Jason whispered, barely audible in the predawn darkness.

"As I'll ever be."

They'd planned carefully—dark clothing, soft-soled shoes, equipment distributed between them in case they got separated. Olive's phone was fully charged with the backup battery pack, camera ready to document whatever they discovered.

They'd talked to Tevin. He was monitoring things from Grayfall. As soon as they found enough evidence, they would text him. He was going to station himself somewhere with cell reception.

When they gave him the go-ahead, he would tell Rex what was happening. Rex would then call the proper authorities and get backup to them.

Moving with practiced stealth, they slipped out of their tent and into the gray twilight that preceded sunrise.

The air was crisp and clean, still holding the lingering smell of last night's campfires. Around them, hundreds of other tents sat silent, their occupants either sleeping off hangovers or simply exhausted by the festival's many disappointments.

They slipped behind the buildings in town, using the trees for cover. Carefully, they crept by the house where Brad was staying. Past the mine entrance. Through more woods.

Finally, they reached the other campsite and paused behind a cluster of trees to survey the area.

This was where the rubber met the road.

Olive breathed a quick prayer for wisdom.

"There." Jason pointed through the trees. "That's where we should go."

The auxiliary buildings.

From their concealed position, Olive saw lights in some of the windows and what appeared to be vehicles parked between the buildings.

Vehicles? The sight of them only confirmed there were other roads leading here.

Maybe that was even why the GPS had messed up on her on the way here.

"Look—it's a line of people headed toward the mountain," Jason murmured. "My guess is that the mine has another entrance."

She watched as probably twenty men dressed in jeans and flannel shirts walked toward the mountain, their steps appearing heavy and burdened.

Her stomach clenched. "You're probably right. It almost looks like forced labor."

"We need to make it to those buildings without being seen."

They watched for several more minutes, waiting for things to settle down in the camp.

"We should go around to the far side." Olive pointed to a route that would keep them in the woods and out of sight until they could approach the buildings from behind. "Those windows are dark—probably storage or empty offices."

"And if we're wrong?" Jason glanced at her.

"Then we improvise." Olive hoped, however, that it wouldn't come to that.

CHAPTER 62

Olive and Jason began working their way around the perimeter of the clearing, moving slowly and carefully to avoid making noise that might carry to the active work areas.

The forest provided good cover, but it also meant they couldn't see what was happening in the buildings until they were close enough to risk being spotted themselves.

As they reached the position Olive had identified, the sound of engines starting up came from the vehicle parking area. Through the trees, they saw trucks beginning to move, headlights cutting through the dawn twilight as a convoy prepared to depart.

Jason recognized the opportunity the vehicle noise provided and said, "Now."

They broke from the woods and darted toward the

nearest building, using the sound of engines and the distraction of the departing convoy to mask their approach. Within seconds, they were pressed against the back wall of what appeared to be an office building.

Olive's heart pounded from the adrenaline of crossing open ground.

Now came the hard part—finding a way inside without being caught.

The question was whether what they found would be worth the enormous risk they were taking to find it.

Olive and Jason darted toward a door at the back of the building.

Jason tried the knob.

It was locked, just as they'd assumed.

He took some picks from his pocket and began to work the mechanism. Finally, it popped.

This was it—their chance to go inside.

They gave each other a look before nodding. Neither was sure what they'd find on the other side of this door.

But they had to know what these buildings were being used for. It was their only hope of finding Chloe and Becca.

Jason opened the door.

Olive held her breath, anxious about what they might find.

A hallway greeted them.

Cautiously, they stepped inside and crept toward the space in the distance. Around them, everything was quiet—no voices or movement. Like the place was empty.

She hoped that was the case.

At the end of the hallway, an office area greeted them—one that was surprisingly vacant.

The space had been completely modernized with computer workstations, secure filing systems, and multiple monitors displaying real-time data feeds from throughout the extraction operation.

"Let's get busy," Jason said. "We need to find any evidence we can to take this operation down."

"Yes, we do."

Olive worked quickly, photographing everything she could while Jason kept watch at the entrance.

The first computer she accessed was logged into a system showing production schedules, shipping manifests, and extraction quotas that represented millions of dollars.

More pieces fell into place as Olive discovered a folder marked "Festival Integration Protocols." The documents inside confirmed what they suspected:

They were using this music festival as a cover for illegal mining operations.

The heavy equipment brought in for "stage construction" was actually extraction machinery. The helicopters that supposedly transported musicians were carrying mining equipment.

But now they knew the truth.

The question was whether they could survive long enough to expose it.

CHAPTER 63

"We need to check the rest of the building," Olive murmured.

"I agree," Jason said. "And we don't know how long we have before anyone comes back here."

"Then let's move fast."

They opened an interior door and scanned the hallway.

Again, it was empty. Everyone must be in the mines right now.

But they didn't know how much longer that would be the case.

As Olive hurried down the hall, she peered through a window in another door.

Her breath caught.

It was Chloe Kingston.

She sat on a narrow cot with her back against the wall in what appeared to be an old executive office.

She was alive!

Relief swept through Olive.

The young woman looked nothing like the vibrant person from the promotional videos. Her designer clothes were torn and stained, her blonde hair hung limp and unwashed, and dark circles under her eyes suggested days without proper sleep.

"Chloe," Olive called softly through the door.

The young woman's head snapped up, her eyes wide with a mixture of hope and disbelief. She struggled to her feet, moving carefully as if every motion caused pain.

"Who's there?" Chloe rushed toward the door, her voice hoarse.

Jason examined the door's lock. "We're here to get you out. Your father hired us to find you."

"My father?" Tears began streaming down Chloe's face. "They told me he didn't know I was missing. They said nobody was looking for me."

"It was another lie," Olive told her.

The lock was a simple deadbolt rather than electronic. Jason had it open in five seconds flat.

As soon as the door opened, Chloe practically collapsed into Olive's arms.

"I thought I was going to die in there." She let out a sob. "They kept asking me what I'd told people, what evidence I'd gathered, who else knew about . . . about what I found."

"What did you find?" Olive supported Chloe's weight as they moved toward the next room.

"The mining operation. During the promotional shoot, I was supposed to film 'behind the scenes' content around the mine entrance for authenticity. But then I found this site and realized what was happening." Chloe's voice strengthened as she talked. "I confronted Brad about it, and that's when everything changed."

That was when Chloe had become a threat, Olive realized. And she had to be dealt with.

The good news was that she was still alive.

The bad news was they still had to get out of here.

Quickly, she texted Tevin. She hoped the message went through in time.

Two rooms down, they found Becca Morrison. The journalism student was in worse condition than Chloe, slumped against the far wall with a grotesquely swollen ankle.

"Becca." Olive threw open the door. "We're getting you out of here."

Becca looked up, squinting as if she was having trouble focusing. "Olivia?"

"It's me. We're here to help."

"I'm so glad to see you. My friend Jessica overheard what they were planning, and they killed her for it." Tears slid from Becca's eyes.

"I'm sorry," Olive told her.

Jason helped Becca to her feet, but her injured ankle couldn't support any weight.

"There are others," Chloe rushed as she stood at the doorway, clearly anxious to get out of here. "An older couple in the room at the end. Local residents who got too close to the truth. And there was a mountain man—the one who was always trying to warn people. They brought him down here yesterday, but I haven't seen him since."

Olive's heart clenched, knowing they'd already found the Guardian's body in the tunnel entrance. But she didn't want to further devastate these women with more bad news.

"We'll check," she said instead, moving toward the remaining rooms with Jason.

The older couple Chloe had mentioned were in the last room—a man and woman in their sixties.

"They own property adjacent to the mountain," Chloe explained as Jason worked on their lock. "They started asking questions when they noticed their well water was contaminated with mining chemicals."

"That's terrible," Olive murmured.

The implications of this were far greater than she'd imagined.

The woman in the room was conscious but seemed to be in shock. Her husband was barely responsive—whether from injury or simple exhaustion, Olive couldn't tell.

"What's your name?" Jason asked as he knelt in front of them.

The woman clutched the man's arm, her face pale. "I'm Margaret, and Carl is my husband."

"How long have you been here?" Olive helped the woman to her feet.

"Three days, maybe four. Hard to tell without sunlight." Margaret's voice grew stronger as she talked. "I thought we were going to die in here! You've got to get us out of here. Please!"

CHAPTER 64

As Jason helped Carl to his feet, the group gathered in the hallway.

"We need to move," Olive murmured. "There's no time to waste."

Two young women, one barely able to walk. An older couple, one of whom could hardly stand. And they still had to navigate the camp area while avoiding security patrols.

As they helped the four rescued captives toward the nearest exit, the sound of voices erupted from the front. Multiple people were entering with the confident stride of those who belonged there.

"We need to prep them for transport within the hour," a deep voice said.

Jason immediately reversed direction, guiding their group away from the approaching voices and toward the offices. But their progress was agonizingly slow—Becca could barely put weight on her swollen ankle, Chloe swayed dangerously with each step as her malnourished body struggled to function, and Margaret was practically carrying Carl, whose legs seemed to give out every few feet.

"This way," Olive whispered, heading toward the exit where she and Jason had entered.

But the voices came closer, and footsteps headed directly toward the area where they'd found the prisoners.

"Discovery in three, two . . ." Jason counted under his breath, knowing that whoever had entered would realize the cells were empty within seconds.

The emergency exit was still twenty feet away when shouts erupted behind them.

"They're gone! All of them! Search the building! Now!"

Olive grabbed Chloe around the waist, half-carrying the younger woman as they stumbled toward the exit. Jason did the same with Carl, while Margaret pushed herself to move faster despite her own exhaustion. Becca hopped desperately on her good foot, using the wall for support.

They shoved the door open and rushed outside.

"Go, go, go," Olive urged, helping Chloe outside while Jason practically carried Carl to ground level.

They'd made it fifty yards into the forest when the emergency door burst open behind them. Armed figures spilled outside and began sweeping the area.

"Keep moving," Jason whispered, though Olive could see the impossibility of their situation written on his face.

They were in dense forest with four people who could barely walk, pursued by armed guards who knew the terrain better than they did. Carl had collapsed against a tree trunk, breathing heavily, while Chloe seemed to be losing consciousness despite Olive's efforts to keep her upright.

"I can't," Becca gasped, her injured ankle finally giving out completely. "I can't go any farther."

Margaret sank to the ground beside her husband, her own strength finally exhausted. "We're slowing you down. You need to go get help."

"We're not leaving anyone behind," Olive said firmly.

But even as she said the words, she had no idea how they were going to get four injured people through miles of mountain forest while being hunted by people with million-dollar secrets to hide.

CHAPTER 65

The men were getting closer, accompanied by radio chatter as the search teams coordinated their pursuit. In the meantime, they stowed everyone behind a cluster of rocks.

It would work—but not for long.

"There has to be another way." Jason studied their surroundings despite the hopelessness of their situation.

Olive pulled out her phone, hoping against hope for enough signal to call for help, but the screen showed nothing. They were cut off, completely on their own.

That was when she heard it—the distant sound of helicopter rotors cutting through the morning air.

"Help or hunting party?" Jason asked, his gaze grim and cautious.

"Only one way to find out." Olive suspected, however, that anyone with access to helicopters in this remote area was probably not on their side.

As the aircraft grew closer and the armed men tightened their net around their position, Olive realized they were facing an impossible choice. Should they surrender and hope for mercy from people who'd already demonstrated their willingness to kill? Or should they continue fleeing through terrain that favored their pursuers while carrying four people who couldn't keep up?

Either way, their chances of survival were dropping rapidly with each passing minute.

The helicopter's rotors grew louder overhead, and Olive found herself hoping that Rex had somehow managed to send backup faster than anyone had thought possible.

Because if he hadn't, they were all about to discover just how far their captors were willing to go to protect their operation.

The helicopter's rotors grew deafeningly loud as it passed overhead.

Through the canopy, Olive caught a glimpse of expensive corporate markings rather than government insignia. This wasn't a rescue crew.

It was leadership arriving to oversee whatever "cleanup" was about to happen.

"We need to move deeper into the forest," Jason said, helping Carl to his feet despite the older man's obvious exhaustion.

They'd made it another hundred or so yards when someone emerged from behind a cluster of pine trees ahead of them.

Olive's breath caught. No . . .

Then she recognized the figure.

Connor Walsh. He stepped into view, his camera bag slung over his shoulder, looking like he'd been hiking through the woods for hours. A confused expression crossed his face as if he didn't expect to see them.

Was he heading from Grayfall to the camp when he'd come across them?

Olive didn't feel certain.

Her guard went up.

Chloe gasped with relief as if she'd just run into her best friend. "Connor, I'm so glad you're here. We need help. They had us locked up, and there are armed guards—"

"I know." Connor sounded strangely calm as he pulled out a radio instead of offering assistance. "Control, this is Walsh. I've located the escaped subjects. Grid reference Charlie-Seven, approximately two hundred meters northeast of Building

Three."

The radio crackled with a response that made Olive's blood turn to ice: "Copy that. Containment teams en route. Maintain visual contact."

CHAPTER 66

"You were a mole this whole time . . ." Jason snarled, immediately positioning himself between Connor and the rest of the group.

Connor's expression was almost apologetic as he clipped the radio back to his belt. "I'm sorry. I really am. But this operation is worth hundreds of millions of dollars, and there are powerful people who won't let a few witnesses destroy it."

"Witnesses to what?" Olive demanded, though she was already calculating distances and options for disarming him. "Environmental crimes? Kidnapping? Murder?"

"To the future of American energy independence," Connor stated, as if that justified everything. "Do you have any idea how much lithium is under this mountain? How much our country needs those resources?"

So it was lithium . . . everything started to click into place.

"So you sell out innocent people for money." Becca's voice shook with pain and betrayal.

"I document the truth." Connor straightened his shoulders. "And the truth is that sometimes sacrifices have to be made for the greater good."

The sound of approaching vehicles echoed through the forest—multiple engines, getting closer fast. Whatever containment teams were responding to Connor's call would be there within minutes.

"Jason," Olive said quietly, her eyes never leaving Connor. She silently urged him to act.

"What are you two up to?" Connor snapped.

Jason moved faster than Connor could react, tackling him to the ground and wrestling for the radio. But Connor was stronger than he looked, and the two men rolled across the forest floor, fighting for control.

The radio went flying into the underbrush as Connor managed to break free from Jason's grip. But instead of running, he reached for something at his belt—a pistol that glinted in the filtered sunlight.

Chloe gasped and drew back.

"Don't make this harder than it has to be," Connor panted, backing away while keeping the gun trained on the group. "The containment teams will be here soon. If you cooperate, maybe they'll make this quick."

"Like they did for the Guardian?" Olive remembered the old man's body in the mine tunnel.

Connor's expression flickered with what might have been genuine remorse. "He shouldn't have interfered. None of you should have."

That moment of distraction was all Jason needed.

He launched himself at Connor again, this time going directly for the gun. The weapon discharged harmlessly into the trees as the two men struggled, but Jason's military training gave him the advantage he needed.

Within seconds, Connor was unconscious on the forest floor, and Jason was checking the pistol's ammunition.

"Six rounds," he reported. "Not much against whatever's coming for us."

The sound of engines came closer now and, through the trees, Olive saw flashes of headlights as vehicles maneuvered the forest roads.

"This way," Carl said suddenly, his voice stronger than it had been since their rescue. "There's an old logging road about a quarter mile north. If they left vehicles there . . ."

CHAPTER 67

Moving as quickly as the group could manage, they followed Carl's directions through dense forest. Behind them, voices shouted as the security team discovered Connor's unconscious form.

The old logging road was exactly where Carl had said it would be, and sitting at the end of it was a vehicle—a rugged SUV that looked capable of handling the mountain terrain. Connor must have joined in the search and driven this here.

"Can you hotwire it?" Olive asked Jason as they reached the vehicle.

"Not my specialty, but I can try." He examined the door locks.

The sound of pursuit came closer. They had

maybe two minutes before security reached their position.

"Margaret." Carl turned to his wife. "Remember when we were dating, and you hotwired your dad's truck because you lost the keys?"

"That was forty years ago, Carl." Margaret shook her head. But, despite her words, she moved toward the driver's side. "Let me try."

Her hands worked with surprising skill, pulling panels and locating wires with the confidence of someone who'd grown up around machinery.

"Come on, come on," she muttered as the sound of pursuit grew louder.

The engine turned over just as the first ATV broke through the trees behind them.

"Got it!" Margaret announced.

Olive jumped behind the wheel as Margaret climbed into the back.

"Go, go, go!" Jason shouted, helping the injured captives into the vehicle as Olive floored the accelerator.

The SUV lurched forward onto the narrow mountain road just as armed figures emerged from the forest, their shouts of frustration echoing through the morning air.

But they weren't safe yet—not even close. They had a head start, but their pursuers had radios, helicopters, and intimate knowledge of every road in the area.

The real challenge was just beginning.

As Olive navigated the winding mountain road, the sound of helicopters grew louder behind them.

But these weren't the corporate aircraft they'd seen earlier—these had the distinctive sound of military rotors, and through the trees, Olive saw multiple helicopters converging on the mining operation.

"Rex came through," Jason said with relief. "Backup is here."

They reached a cliff about two miles from the mining site, where Olive finally stopped the SUV.

From their position, they could see the entire operation spread out below them—the festival grounds, the mine entrance, and the cluster of buildings where they'd been held prisoner.

Federal agents swarmed the area like ants, their vehicles creating a perimeter around the entire site while helicopters landed in the festival's main area. Even from this distance, Olive could see people being detained, equipment being secured, and what appeared to be a coordinated takedown of the entire operation.

Maybe this was over.

She wanted to feel relieved. But something stopped her.

"Olive." Jason handed her his binoculars. "You should see this."

CHAPTER 68

Through the lenses, Olive saw men moving around what appeared to be a makeshift landing pad beside the camp. A sleek corporate helicopter sat on the cleared ground, its rotors beginning to spin as several well-dressed figures hurried toward it.

These weren't the miners or security personnel they'd encountered.

These people wore expensive suits and moved with the confident urgency of executives trying to escape a collapsing situation.

"The real power behind the operation . . ." Olive adjusted the focus to get a clearer view.

One figure turned toward the approaching federal agents, and even at this distance, something about his bearing made Olive's breath catch. The way he carried himself, the arrogant posture, the graying hair that caught the morning light—

"It can't be." Her hands trembled as she gripped the binoculars tighter.

The man was older now, more distinguished, his hair completely silver rather than the dark brown she remembered. But there was no mistaking the features, the confident stance, the way he gestured to the other figures as if accustomed to being obeyed.

Mr. Henderson. The wealthy businessman who'd been so charmed by her father's treasure hunting stories during that camping trip eleven years ago.

He was involved with this? How was that even possible?

Part of her didn't even want to consider the possibilities.

"What is it?" Jason asked, noting her sudden tension. "Did you see something I didn't?"

Olive couldn't speak, couldn't process what she was seeing.

The man who'd seemed like such a kind, curious tourist—who'd asked so many questions about her father's research methods, who'd been so interested in investing in future expeditions—was climbing into the helicopter with the other executives fleeing the scene.

"Olive, what's wrong?" Chloe asked from the back seat, her voice weak.

"I just saw someone I know," Olive managed to say, though the words felt inadequate. "Someone from a long time ago."

Through the binoculars, she watched as Henderson seemed to look directly at their position, as if he could sense her watching him. For just a moment, their eyes seemed to meet across the distance, and she saw him smile—the same charming, confident smile that had won over her family during that camping trip.

Then he disappeared into the helicopter, and the aircraft lifted off just as federal agents reached the landing area. The sleek machine rose quickly, banking away from the mountain and disappearing over the ridge before anyone could stop it.

"They got away," Jason said as he watched the helicopter's departure.

"The big fish always do," Carl added with the bitter wisdom of someone who'd spent years investigating environmental crimes. "The feds will shut down this operation and arrest the workers and security personnel. But the people who funded it will just move to another location and start over."

Olive wanted to argue with his words.

But she couldn't.

Mostly because he was entirely correct.

CHAPTER 69

Olive lowered the binoculars, her mind reeling with implications she wasn't ready to fully process. Henderson's presence here wasn't a coincidence—it couldn't be. His interest in her father's treasure hunting expeditions suddenly took on a completely different meaning.

Had that camping trip been a planning session disguised as a family adventure?

And if so, what did that mean about her family's murder? About the house in Oasis that was now owned by a shell company? About all the questions she'd been afraid to ask Jason about his father's business connections?

"We need to get these people to a hospital." Jason's voice cut through her racing thoughts. "And we need to make sure our evidence gets to the right people."

Olive nodded, forcing herself to focus on the immediate needs of the people they'd rescued. But as she put the SUV into Drive and they began the descent toward civilization, she couldn't shake the image of Henderson's smile—or the terrible certainty that this was far from over.

Her gut told her that the man who'd escaped in that helicopter knew exactly who she was. And now he knew she'd survived long enough to connect him to this operation.

Which meant that everyone she cared about—including Jason—was now in danger from an enemy who'd been planning his moves for over a decade.

The Grayfall Festival grounds looked like the aftermath of a natural disaster.

Federal agents moved methodically through the campsite, documenting evidence and taking statements, while confused festivalgoers packed their belongings with the bewildered efficiency of people who still couldn't quite process what had happened to their weekend getaway.

In the distance, the members of Obscurity were setting up their equipment on the makeshift stage—

apparently no one had thought to tell them that their headlining performance was now completely irrelevant. The surreal sound of a proper sound check drifted across the ruins of what had been an elaborate criminal conspiracy.

Olive sat on a fallen log near the old mercantile building, her laptop open as she coordinated with Rex via satellite phone. Tevin sat beside her, uploading encrypted files to Aegis servers, while Jason stood guard with the casual alertness of someone who'd learned not to trust apparent safety.

"Forensic teams are processing the mine," Rex's voice crackled through the speaker. "Initial estimates suggest this operation extracted more than fifty million dollars' worth of lithium and rare earth elements. We're tracking shell companies across six states now."

"What about the helicopter?" Olive asked, though she already suspected the answer.

"Gone. But we'll find them eventually—operations this size leave paper trails."

Olive hoped that was the truth. But a measure of doubt still lingered inside her.

CHAPTER 70

Across the campsite, Chloe Kingston sat wrapped in a blanket beside Tristan Pembroke, who looked like he'd aged five years in the past twenty-four hours. He'd told them her father was sending a helicopter for her.

Maya Riggs was, predictably, documenting everything for her social media followers, though her tone had shifted from influencer enthusiasm to genuine journalism. "This is probably the most insane story I'll ever tell," she'd said while setting up her camera. "My followers are not going to believe this."

Dr. Z—whose real name turned out to be Dr. Martin Zimmerman—sat on the curb with a calculator, apparently trying to figure out how much money he'd lost.

The local sheriff, a weathered man in his sixties named Patterson, was clearly in over his head trying to coordinate the evacuation of several hundred disappointed festivalgoers while federal agents processed a major crime scene around them.

"Most folks just want to get home and pretend this never happened," he'd told Olive. "Can't say I blame them."

Neither could she.

She glanced at the woods above the town. She no longer saw the Dark Watchers there. Maybe they really were townspeople trying to protect this place but feeling voiceless. When Chloe said, "The trees are watching," she must have meant the people in the woods. The forest did feel like it had its eyes on everything.

Perhaps that was what had happened to those missing hikers as well. They'd stumbled somewhere they hadn't been welcomed. They'd paid the price with their lives.

Their bodies had been found buried in the woods close to the migrant camp.

Just then, someone else caught Olive's eye.

Someone she really wanted to speak with.

She excused herself and headed across the grounds.

Elias Mercer stood near the food tent, speaking with a federal investigator who took detailed notes. The lodge owner looked like a man who'd been carrying a terrible burden and was finally able to set it down.

"I agreed to help host people and get them to Grayfall," she heard him saying as she approached. "They said it was just a music festival, maybe a little unconventional, but legitimate. I had no idea all of this was going on."

"But you suspected something," the investigator pressed.

"Toward the end, yes. The organizer was very pushy, very controlling. When I tried to back out of the arrangement, things at the lodge would get sabotaged. Equipment would break, supplies would go missing. The message was clear—cooperate or suffer the consequences."

"And Connor Walsh was your primary contact?"

"Him and a few others. But Connor was the one who made it clear what would happen if I didn't cooperate." Elias's voice carried genuine regret. "I should have called the authorities, but they made it seem like I was already too deep in to get out clean."

The investigator made a few more notes, then moved away to interview other witnesses. Olive approached Elias, who looked up at her with the weary recognition of someone who'd been expecting this conversation.

"Could I have a moment alone with you?" Olive asked.

The investigator nodded, and Olive sat beside Elias.

"You were at the lodge twenty years ago," Olive said without preamble. "There's a photograph in your main room showing a corporate retreat. Northwoods Investment Group."

Elias's expression grew guarded. "That was a long time ago."

"My father was in that photograph. James Sterling. Do you remember him?"

Recognition immediately crossed Elias's face, along with other more complicated emotions—surprise, wariness, and maybe even sadness.

"James Sterling," he said. "Yes, I remember him. Brilliant man. Charming, knowledgeable."

"What was the Northwoods Investment Group?"

He shrugged. "Honestly, I don't know. I wasn't privy to that information, and they were so secretive about things."

"You really had no idea?"

"I had the impression they were some kind of development group. But everyone involved seemed successful and like good businessmen. They met here every year for three years. Then I never heard from them again."

"Do you remember who any of the other men were?"

"Some of them. Businessmen, investors. One was named Henderson. He was about your father's age. Very well-dressed, seemed to be in charge." Elias's expression darkened. "And now I understand why they were so interested in this area."

Olive nodded, pieces of the puzzle finally beginning to form a coherent picture.

But how did her father fit into this?

And what did this mean about the shell company that now owned her family's house, about Jason's father's possible connections to the conspiracy, about all the secrets that were still buried beneath decades of careful planning?

As Obscurity launched into their first song in the background—a perfectly executed performance for an audience that was mostly federal agents and crime scene technicians—Olive realized that solving the mystery of Chloe Kingston's disappearance had only opened the door to much larger questions about her own family's fate.

Questions that someone had been willing to kill to keep buried.

And now that person knew she was still alive, still asking questions, still searching for the truth.

The real investigation was just beginning. Maybe

it was time she used some of her personal leave to find the answers that had been just out of reach for so long.

She looked over at Jason as he talked to one of the cops. His gaze met hers, and her cheeks flushed as she remembered the conversations they'd had this week.

Soon, she would have to decide. She couldn't keep him hanging for too long.

She took a step toward him when someone called her name.

She turned and saw Tevin standing there, an odd look on his face.

"Are you okay?" She stepped closer, concern filling her.

Usually, they had more opportunities to chat and catch up while working these cases. She'd missed having that time with him on this case, but it just hadn't been possible.

He stuffed his hands into his pockets, appearing strangely nervous. "Don't choose him."

She blinked, uncertain she'd understood him correctly. "What?"

"Jason." He nodded at Jason. "Don't pick him."

Her heart beat harder. "What do you mean?"

Tevin reached forward and touched her arm. "Pick me, Olive. I've loved you since the day we met.

I've just been too afraid of ruining our friendship to tell you."

She opened her mouth then closed it again. "I don't understand."

He came closer. "If I didn't tell you this now, then I knew I would always regret it. But Olive, the two of us are perfect together. You and I both know it. I'd make you happier than he would. So pick me."

He stared at her with such sincerity in his gaze.

This wasn't a joke. Tevin meant the words.

He loved her.

Maybe she should have seen it. Seen it in the lingering looks he'd given her. The way he was always available. The way all his other relationships only lasted a few dates.

She'd thought of him like a brother, someone she could tell her secrets to and kick back to relax with. He was one of her best friends.

She loved his obsession with all things dill-pickle-flavored. How he called his mom almost every day. How he was both a computer nerd and an athlete.

But . . . could there be more between them? She'd never even considered the idea.

Olive glanced at Jason again. Then at Tevin.

She licked her lips as she tried to figure out what to say.

~~~

Thank you for reading ***Obscurity***. If you enjoyed this book, please consider leaving a review.

Coming next: Enigma.

~~~

ALSO BY CHRISTY BARRITT:

THE LANTERN BEACH SERIES

LANTERN BEACH MYSTERIES

When a notorious gang puts a bounty on Detective Cady Matthews's head, she has no choice but to hide until she can testify at trial. But her temporary home across the country on a remote North Carolina island isn't as peaceful as she initially thinks. Living under the new identity of Cassidy Livingston, she struggles to keep her investigative skills tucked away. One wrong move could lead to both her discovery and her demise.

Hidden Currents
Flood Watch
Storm Surge

Dangerous Waters
Perilous Riptide
Deadly Undertow

LANTERN BEACH ROMANTIC SUSPENSE

Books in the Romantic Suspense series are standalone and do not need to be read in order. Each features a pulse-pounding story centered around a resident of Lantern Beach. Some come to Lantern beach to heal, some are running from their pasts. All are in peril.

Tides of Deception
Shadow of Intrigue
Storm of Doubt
Winds of Danger
Rains of Remorse
Torrents of Fear

LANTERN BEACH PD

When a cult moves to Lantern Beach, Police Chief Cassidy Chambers must act quickly to prevent chaos. The more Cassidy learns about the seemingly untouchable Gilead's Cove community, the more her unease grows. The problem is that Cassidy's pool of suspects gets deeper every day. Cassidy is determined to protect the island and break up the cult . . . but the cult's growing threat could lead to the pinnacle standoff of good versus evil.

On the Lookout
Attempt to Locate
First Degree Murder
Dead on Arrival
Plan of Action

LANTERN BEACH BLACKOUT

Join a group of Navy SEALs who've come to Lantern Beach, North Carolina, to start an elite private security firm. As they protect the innocent, the Blackout team must fight for justice and uncover dark secrets hiding beneath seemingly still waters.

Dark Water
Safe Harbor
Ripple Effect
Rising Tide

LANTERN BEACH GUARDIANS

During a turbulent storm, a child is found on the

beach, washed up from the ocean. Making matters worse, the girl can't speak. Lantern Beach Police Chief Cassidy Chambers can feel the danger lurking around them. Someone appears to be playing a deadly version of hide-and-seek, using the girl as a pawn. Cassidy and her husband, Ty, will do anything to protect the child, each other, and the island. But what happens when they might not be able to save all three?

Hide and Seek
Shock and Awe
Safe and Sound

LANTERN BEACH BLACKOUT: THE NEW RECRUITS

Four new recruits join Blackout and are drawn into sinister circumstances. As the ex-Navy SEALs tackle their risky assignments, it's not only their lives that are on the line, it's also their hearts. As trouble finds the women they are tasked to protect, danger escalates and one thing becomes clear: there's no room for error.

Rocco
Axel
Beckett

Gabe

LANTERN BEACH MAYDAY

Med student Kenzie Anderson, tired of letting others chart her future, accepts a job as second steward aboard a luxury yacht. But when she finds the captain dead, she wonders if she's in over her head. The new captain, Jimmy James, joins her in figuring out how to stop a killer before anyone else is hurt. As they set out to sea, Kenzie and Jimmy James realize the yacht they are working on seems to be a magnet for murder and mayhem, leading them both into a tumultuous seafaring journey neither of them expected.

Run Aground
Dead Reckoning
Tipping Point

LANTERN BEACH BLACKOUT: DANGER RISING

A new team is formed to combat a new enemy. They must infiltrate a dangerous organization known as The System and uncover their deadly plans that could destroy thousands of lives. The new Blackout agents are the only ones who can stop what's about to be unleashed. The mission puts everyone on the line, and failure would mean chaos . . . not only for them but for their nation.

Brandon
Dylan
Maddox
Titus

ABOUT THE AUTHOR

USA Today has called Christy Barritt's books "scary, funny, passionate, and quirky."

Christy writes both mystery and romantic suspense novels that are clean with underlying messages of faith. Her books have sold more than five million copies and have won the Daphne du Maurier Award for Excellence in Suspense and Mystery, have been twice nominated for the Romantic Times Reviewers' Choice Award, and have finaled for both a Carol Award and Foreword Magazine's Book of the Year.

She is married to her Prince Charming, a man who thinks she's hilarious—but only when she's not trying to be. Christy is a self-proclaimed klutz, an avid music lover who's known for spontaneously bursting into song, and a road trip aficionado.

When she's not working or spending time with her family, she enjoys singing, playing the guitar, and exploring small, unsuspecting towns where people have no idea how accident-prone she is.

Find Christy online at:

www.christybarritt.com
www.facebook.com/christybarritt
www.twitter.com/cbarritt

Sign up for Christy's newsletter to get information on all of her latest releases here: **www.christybarritt.com/newsletter-sign-up/**

facebook.com / AuthorChristyBarritt
x.com / christybarritt
instagram.com / cebarritt

www.ingramcontent.com/pod-product-compliance
Lightning Source LLC
LaVergne TN
LVHW092100130925
820963LV00009B/152